# ORIGINS

*a novella by*

## AUGUST HEI

# CONTENTS

To my readers,

For joining me on this journey,

And the many journeys to come.

# CHAPTER 1: A SPOONFUL OF SOUP

I stared at the man with my brows raised and my mouth hung open and my soup-filled spoon paused just below my chin. I had not noticed him in the dining hall when we took our seats, but now he stood beside our table, capturing all my attention. He was perhaps seventy years of age. He wore a frayed apron over a simple tunic. A half-tucked washcloth spilled from a side pocket on his trousers. A tray with two plates of chicken and potatoes, still steaming with hot gravy, was held in his calloused hands. His face was lined with the markings of a long hard life, but at this moment, it held an open expression of wonder that almost made him look youthful.

"It's you," he said again, and tears began welling at the corners of his eyes.

My brows rose further now and my eyes squinted with confusion. But my mouth was still hanging open and my soup spoon hung in the air. I'd not had one bite of the hot meal thus far, and my stomach growled in protest. Behind me, someone barked a laugh, followed by a bout of giggling. No doubt it was the table with the two women and the man with the sharp face and still sharper eyes. At the corner of my vision, I noticed that Charm had gone on eating her meal as if there wasn't an old man tearing up beside our table with big shining eyes.

"I beg your pardon?" I finally managed, deciding the spoonful of soup could wait despite the fact I hadn't had proper food in a fortnight.

"I don't believe it, it's really you," the old man said, the tears now streaking down his cheeks. Then a sudden look of embarrassment came over his face and he dropped to one knee, setting the tray on the ground. "Where are my manners? It is a great honor to see you again, Archibold...don." He held a hand to his chest, beaming at me. "You must not recognize me. I'm Torren, Torren Goodland, the baker's son in Roundtree—I used to play with Lily and the others. Do you remember?"

For a moment, I forgot about my soup entirely. "Uhh... I'm sorry, good sir, but you seem to have confused me for another very handsome man." I held up a hand. "No need to apologize, it's my fault my striking good looks are the conventional sort."

It was Torren's turn to look confused. He opened his mouth to say something, but was cut off by the arrival of the innkeeper, a barrel of a woman with plump cheeks, and humor-laden eyes, but at this moment they were rather filled with horror.

"What in the Abyss are you doing with the tray on the floor, Grandda?" She swooped down and snatched up the food. "And what're you kneeling for?"

Torren was still in a daze, but his features took on a look of uncertainty and embarrassment that old men sometimes have when they've done something foolish around the young.

"I'm sorry, Tammy," Torren mumbled. "I forgot myself. The plates are still clean, only the tray touched the ground."

"Did you fall again, Grandda?" Tammy said with a look of worry.

"No... I-" Torren began, but seemed unable to find the right words to complete his thoughts as he gave me a quick glance.

"Why don't you go take a seat in the kitchen and have the cook make you something to eat," Tammy suggested.

Torren nodded, looking abashed. He gave me one low bow before heading off to the kitchen.

"You'll have to forgive him, dear," Tammy said to me, still carrying the tray of chicken and potatoes. "It's a terrible thing to get old. My grandda used to be as strong as a wurtbull." There was a moment of sadness in her voice before she smiled. "Anything else I can get you two?"

"Oh uh, no we're alright," I said, aching to get back to my soup. But then a thought occurred to me. "Actually, do you carry any ales?"

The innkeeper's grin grew wide, an excitement taking over her features. "Do we? You've come to the right place if you want ales, friend! We have the Blended Wheat, Cherry Purple, Red Harvest, Oatmeal Stout, and the Dirty Apple Cider." Upon seeing my confusion, she added, "My favorite's the Red Harvest. The Tree and Stump Company does a fine job with their amber."

"I'll take one of those," I said. "Thank you."

"Right away. Anything for the lady?"

For the first time since we sat down, Charm looked up from her meal, turning her flat eyes to the innkeeper. "Nothing for me, but please pass my compliments to your chef. The stew is quite pleasing."

The innkeeper blinked. "Thank you, young lady. I shall, and I'll be right back with that Red Harvest once I drop off these plates."

I took a deep breath as I watched the innkeeper serve the chicken plates to the table down the hall. Then I broke apart the bread on my plate and scooped a new spoonful of soup that was likely lukewarm instead of hot by now. But before I could raise the inviting broth to my lips, Charm said in a low tone, "We've not made it two steps into the city and you've already been recognized. Would this be an opportune time to remind you of your plan's staggering stupidity?"

"No, this wouldn't be a good time," I snapped under my breath, and I dropped the spoon back in the soup. "The decision has already been made, and there's no point arguing it again."

"And when you are recognized again?" Charm said without looking in my direction as she precisely scooped up the remains of her bowl. She was nearly done with her meal and I'd barely begun to eat mine.

"It was a fluke," I replied. "Best we not dwell on it." Despite my words, I had the terrible feeling that fate was toying with me. What were the chances I'd be recognized upon entering the city? One to a million? What were the chances I'd be recognized at all anywhere in Visseria?

"Explain," Charm said, and I knew she meant she wanted to know who Torren was and how he knew me.

I looked over at the kitchen, and through the cloth curtain that partially covered its entrance, I could see Torren sitting at a small table, drinking something hot from a mug.

"I'll tell you about it later," I said, raising the soup to my mouth once more.

"Don't do that," said a new voice. Rough but strong. A dangerous voice.

I looked up and saw the sharp-eyed, sharp-faced man. He was grinning and his knife-like eyes sunk into mine as he pulled a chair from a nearby table to ours. He sat down, with the chair back against our table and his scarred muscular arms propped on the seat rest.

"I'd like to hear the story as well. Not often you see a grown man getting to his knees. Not for a young lad like you who has spent no more than a year as a man, which means you must be someone very interesting, and I *enjoy* meeting interesting people." The man's grin widened, but his eyes were anything but friendly.

Ho
Slurp...

# CHAPTER 2: DEEP TROUBLE

"E r... I beg your pardon?"

"Tell me the story. The one you were planning to tell her later." He gestured in Charm's direction with his head, still grinning, but his voice had taken on a small perceptible edge.

"Y-you want to hear the s-story?" I stammered.

"That's right." The man leaned forward from his perch.

"B-but it's a very private story, and we haven't been acquainted yet."

"The name is Sard," he said easily and held out his hand. "Pleasure to meet you."

With some hesitation, I accepted his hand, taking note of the layered scars across his knuckles. "Arch Gustkin."

"What do you know? We're acquainted." Sard's grip tightened. "Now how about that story, Gustkin?"

"I-I don't know..."

"If you're afraid I can't keep a secret, don't be. You can ask around. I'm as tight-lipped as they come."

"Okay, let me ask around," I said, rising.

"Sit down," Sard said, pulling me back into my seat with his grip. The grin had left his face. "Ask later. But I assure you, I take care of my friends. My enemies, not so much. Thankfully, my enemies don't tend to stick around for very long."

He was giving me one of those confident menacing looks, and his grip on my hand had tightened again to the point that it was plenty uncomfortable. The look on his face suggested he could take it even further if he deemed it necessary.

I swallowed. "How about acquaintances? How do you treat them?"

Something in Sard's features turned cold. "Tell me that story, or don't. Choose now, boy."

I noticed that the sounds of the inn continued around us, but they had changed in tune, becoming delicate and practiced. I saw that everyone had turned away from us, their faces focused on each other and their meals. Even Tammy, who had been in and out of the kitchen and drifting between the tables, was nowhere to be found. Sard was not only dangerous, he was infamous.

I looked down at my soup and took a deep breath, nodding. "Okay, I'll tell you if you must know."

"Attaboy," Sard said, releasing me and resting his arms on the seatback.

I looked at him, then looked away again, unable to maintain eye contact. "It um... occurred a while back... I can't be sure from where... y'know, it can be hard to place such things, but it was definitely an accident!" I shot Charm a meaningful glance.

Sard furrowed his brows, looking like he failed to understand.

"Err..." I began again. "There was a barmaid at this inn we stopped by a couple weeks back. A fine young woman. Not that I was attracted to her or anything. I barely spoke to the lovely lady, I swear. But any man would take a glance at a voluptuous beauty like that, young or old, red-blooded or not."

"What does this have to do with anything?" Sard growled.

"You're right! Viola has nothing to do with it! Nothing at all! She's too perfect for such things. A-nd in any case I-I barely talked to her." I lowered my voice. "So I'm thinking... I mean, I'm certain it was the latrine seat at the inn. It has to be. The innkeeper must not have cleaned it right, probably because he'd been too busy keeping his eye on Viola rather than on his business and the hygiene of his latrine seats."

Sard was more confused than mad, his eyes squinted and mouth parted, looking much like I had minutes earlier with Torren. Charm looked away and shook her head imperceptibly.

"What!?" I snapped at her. "I'm telling the truth! You don't know how hard it is being a man! We accidentally touch against things all the time! How is it my fault that the latrine seat happened to be covered in some horrible disease that turns your skin black and scaly, with a thick green ooze that—"

My body lurched forward—Sard had grabbed my collar and pulled my face to his. "What in Celeru's deep Abyss are you saying!"

"Gyah!" I threw up my hands with a whimper. "You're right! It was Viola who gave me the rash all along! I'm sorry for lying!"

Sard threw me back into my chair. "That's not the story I asked for!"

I peeked past my raised arms. "But you said you wanted the story I was about to tell my companion."

"No," Sard hissed through gritted teeth and pointed toward the kitchen. "I want to know why that man got on his knees for you."

"Oh that?" I said, my shoulders visibly relaxing. "That was just a misunderstanding. The innkeeper said I reminded him of some childhood friend. Wait a minute... are you saying I didn't need to tell you about the rash on my grapes!?"

Sard watched me for a long moment, and I noticed the inn had turned completely silent. Apparently everyone had heard my outburst. But Sard ignored the silence, ignored the attention on us from the rest of the inn, and kept his careful eyes on me. Finally, he said, "I saw you when you came in, and I knew right then there was something wrong about you. I wasn't quite sure what it was until now. You looked too comfortable when you came in. Didn't even glance in my direction. Didn't bat an eye when I joined you at your table. Even now I don't sense fear in you. None at all. You've been lying the moment you entered this inn, haven't you?"

"Wha-wha-what a-are y-you s-saying?" I said, my hands trembling as I pushed myself away from him.

"There's no point in feigning it now!" Sard said with a measure of annoyance. But then he grinned at me again and leaned forward, his features returned to being menacing, only this time, his eyes were filled with unveiled curiosity. "Tell me who you are."

"I-I told you, I'm Arch Gustkin."

"What's your business in Meritas?"

"I'm um... here to open a tavern."

"A tavern?" Sard said, his brows rising with a look of disbelief.

I looked from him to Charm who had been watching our interaction with her unreadable eyes. I whispered to her. "Hey, how would you explain what a tavern is to someone who's never heard of one?"

"Much like an inn," Charm said in that unique accent of hers. "But without the primary purpose of room and board. A place to eat and drink."

Sard slammed his fist on the table. "I know what a tavern is, damn you!"

"Oh no, why is he getting angry?" I whispered urgently to Charm.

"He thinks you've insulted his intelligence," she replied.

"What, is he an idiot? I've done no such thing."

Sard launched out of his seat, lifting me by the collar with both hands until our noses were nearly touching. I stared back into his glaring eyes with exasperation.

Then, just as suddenly, he released me and turned to his female companions. "Let's go girls, we're leaving."

"Why? He doesn't look like nobody important," said one of them.

He didn't reply, and stepped out of the inn into the night, letting the door close behind him. The two women shared a look and quickly hurried after him.

I let out a sigh. "First he's furious, then he's about to kiss me. What a strange guy."

Charm's flat gaze had not changed, but somehow I could tell she didn't find my comment amusing. Neither did Tammy who had reappeared at our table. Her features were grim as she set down the mug of ale I'd ordered earlier and turned her gaze from the door to me. "Do you know who that was?"

I shook my head.

"Put it simply, he's a man best never known. Too late for that now. What did Sard want from you?"

"I don't know..." I said, scratching my head. "It was all very confusing. One moment he's asking me about my rash, the next moment he's all angry and wants to know why Torren was kneeling."

Tammy bit her lip. "That's bad news for us both, then. I know you two aimed to stay three nights, but you'd better move on first thing in the morning." She looked back at the door and shook her head as lines of worry deepened across her forehead. "Til the day I die," she mumbled.

"Miss Innkeeper," Charm said in a way that seemed to break Tammy away from her dark thoughts.

"Yes, ma'am?"

"Who is this Sard?"

"He works for Harkness." Then, from the look on our faces, she said, "First time in the city?"

Charm and I both nodded.

"They call him the Silent Boss. Harkness isn't a don like Urindal, but he does business with them. As he does with the duke and many of the noble houses. He doesn't have any territory, but he's got his fingers dipped in a third of the city. Some say most of it is legitimate, and some say most of it isn't." Tammy paused and shook her head. "From what I've seen, he'll use both ways against you."

"Who's the Urinal guy you mentioned?" I said when she did not add more.

"Urindal," the innkeeper said. "He runs Yumentown and pretty much all of Meritas' underworld for that matter. Although there's been some rumors of a new challenger, I don't know much about it."

"The duke allows crime lords to exist in the city?" Charm said.

"Not much he can do. Gave up on regulating Yumentown a long time ago. Of course the Watch Commander, Lord Mackeries wants Urindal's head, but the don hasn't been caught yet. And they say he's got mages with gates to match the duke's. But ol' Urindal knows the rules. He keeps the crime off the main streets and out of the commercial wards, and so the nobles aren't much incentivised to go after him."

"Hmm..." I scratched my chin. "So which wards are not under these crime people's influence? We're looking to buy a tavern and start a business... best avoid such personalities, I think."

"Wise question, but a tavern house won't be a cheap purchase in the wards Urindal stays out of. That's Angelmore, Lumitra, Quell hills, and the like. I suppose you could try Keeper's Garden or Southbank, but can't say I know that part of the city well. Just remember this, even if Urindal stays out of the noble's wards, Harkness doesn't. He'll operate anywhere if there's coin to be made."

"Thank you for the information, Ms. Innkeeper," Charm said. "Your wisdom of the city is much appreciated."

Tammy smiled. "Not at all. I'm sorry to be sending you two along, but it's better that way. If Sard's keen on you, you're bound to end up in trouble. If he asks about you two, I'll say you mentioned meeting a friend in Angelmore. That ought to have him leave you alone. Tell you what, if you're thinking about visiting Keeper's Garden, you can try out Sharla's Inn. Tell her Tammy and Torren sent you. She'll give you a good rate."

"Thank you," I said, grinning back at her. In the pause before anyone said anything else, my stomach made an angry growl.

"My, you haven't eaten yet, have you? Must be starving."

"Sure am," I said, chuckling and picking up my spoon again. But before I could get a scoop of broth, Tammy pulled the bowl away from me.

"Let me get you a fresh one," she said. "This one's already cold."

I was so hungry, temperature was the least of my concerns, but Tammy had already disappeared into the kitchen before I could make any protest.

"Why does it feel like I'm never going to get a taste of that soup?" I said to Charm.

"The costs of being a talkative fool," she replied.

I felt a hard tug in my chest and rubbed it, giving Charm a frown. Luckily, I still had the bread that'd come with the soup on my plate and I took a bite of it. It was crunchy on the outside and soft and doughy on the inside, buttery but lightly sweet, a taste and texture that flooded my senses with nostalgia. How many years had it been since I'd had bread such as this? I swallowed and dared not look in the kitchen's direction again.

Finding somewhere else to look, I rested my eyes on the mug of ale Tammy had brought out earlier.

I knew drinking on an empty stomach wasn't a good idea given my current mortal state, but my stomach was still growling and the amber liquid in the mug seemed to whisper my name.

I sniffed the bubbling gasses and discovered soft, sweet aromas. Then I raised the mug to my lips and took a sip. I swallowed down one large gulp, then another, and then another, and more and more, until the entire mug was emptied.

Charm raised a brow at me and I slammed the mug down on the table. "I've just come to the terrible conclusion that we are in grave trouble!"

"You have received the attentions of a crime lord?"

"Don't be silly," I said and tapped soberly on my emptied mug. "We've got fierce competition in this city. This ale is absolutely delicious!"

# CHAPTER 3: AUTHORITY

Our room at the inn overlooked the stables and backyard. It fit two small beds against opposing walls with a wide enough space in between for the door to open and close without being hampered. An oil lamp sat on the dresser between the beds near the window. I entered after Charm and went to the window to light the oil lamp and get a look of our wagon that had been stationed behind the inn. I had set runes that would notify me of tampering as long as I was close enough, but all my brewing equipment was in the wagon and I worried for its safety. Happily, the wagon looked just as we left it, and I saw no movement in the yard's night shadows.

"You have a story to tell," Charm said, and I turned to find her seated on her bed, pressing her traveling dress neatly across her legs. She gave me an arch of the brow.

"Right, Torren," I said with a deep breath and sat down across from her on my own bed. But before I began to explain, I found myself surprised to be here with her in this room, in this inn, staring at her youthful face, framed by her pink hair that fell past her shoulders along her simple traveling clothes. For a moment, she looked like the young traveler, who had journeyed south across leagues of forest and hills to find better fortunes with her companion. But the darkness in her eyes reminded me otherwise.

I rubbed my chest, feeling a supernatural coldness there. "He grew up in the same village as Camellia... he was the baker's son and Lily's friend."

"He saw you often?"

"No. Just a few times. I didn't visit much toward the end. But a bandit troop came through when they were teenagers. The bandits killed many, including his parents."

"I assume the great Stormblood defeated the bandits and saved the village."

"Something like that," I said, looking away, but I could feel Charm's intent gaze on me.

"Do you realize how vulnerable we are?"

"It'll be fine," I said, feeling my irritation returning. "I can count on my hands the number of people still alive who can recognize me."

"I don't think you comprehend what has happened. What you've done has defied the rhythms of nature. That is why fate has brought you and Torren together."

"I never took you for the superstitious type."

"This is not superstition," Charm said, and I noted that her voice had turned icy.

"There's no one else in this city that will recognize me, Charm. I promise."

Charm frowned. It was unusual to see an expression on her face. "I hate that name."

"What, Charm?" *This is a new complaint*, I thought. "What's wrong with it?" I said. "I think it's cute."

Charm's gaze deadened, nearing on being murderous. I smiled back at her.

"It's one thing to call me that when we are alone. Another in front of others. It makes me sound like a little girl who spends her time reading amorous books and picking flowers."

"Good," I said. "Because reading books and picking flowers is exactly the sort of thing we'll be doing in our free time from now on. Assuming we have any free time given the work ahead of us, but you get my point. You're Charm, and I'm Arch. Those are our identities now."

"It will not last. Cannot."

"That's precisely why I defied the rhythms of nature, or whatever you want to call it."

I could tell she vehemently disagreed that my solution would work. I sighed. "Charm, haven't you ever wondered what it's like to be one of them?" I held up my hand before she could retort. "I mean truly one of them."

"Why wonder about the impossible?"

I smiled tiredly at her. "Usually the impossible things are the most worthy things to wonder about." Then I blinked, realizing that the sentence had come from a memory centuries old.

Charm did not reply nor say anything else to me after that. We sat in silence for a long while, as all the words and arguments had already been said many times before. After a while, Charm got up and began unpacking a few things from her bag. We took turns using the washroom at the end of the hall. Then we got into our beds and I blew out the oil lamp.

As I lay in bed, I felt her soul tugging against mine, turning my chest cold even more than it had before. She was testing my authority as her master, threatening to overturn it, to exchange our roles. But I held strong, unwilling to diverge from the decisions already made.

# CHAPTER 4: A BITE OF EGGS

Torren was downstairs at the clerk's counter when Charm and I came down the stairs the next morning. He seemed to be waiting for me as he stood and straightened upon seeing me, giving me a warm smile and a wave. He looked refreshed this morning, almost like a different man. "How did you sleep... sir?"

"Good, thank you," I said, feeling uneasy about seeing him again. But I had to settle the bill for the stay, and so there was no escape.

"I apologize for last night," Torren said. "I did not mean to cause trouble for you and your companion."

"No trouble at all," I said. "Your granddaughter runs an excellent inn. You must be very proud."

Torren nodded, smiling again. "That she does."

"What do I owe you for the room?"

Torren shook his head. "There is no charge. I will not say more, other than it has brought me great joy to see you. Please come visit any time."

I sighed. "I can't see why you wouldn't charge me. I ate at your inn and stayed the night."

"Consider it the strange predilections of a senile old man," Torren said with a smile. "I've already brought your wagon around. Please have a safe trip, may many good fortunes shine upon you."

"Thank you," I said and set the room key on the counter. Beside me, Charm gave a bow, and then we stepped out the front door.

Tammy was sweeping the area outside her inn. She nodded to us, but something was different about her this morning. Her cheerful manner was replaced by a look of uncertainty.

"Thank you for the stay and the guidance," I said as we walked by. Turtle, who was not a turtle but a horse, snorted as he eyed me. He looked well taken care of, his coat brushed and his hooves cleaned. Torren's handiwork, I guessed.

"My grandda wouldn't tell me who he thinks you are," Tammy said from behind me. She had stopped sweeping but held her broomstick close. A small frown was on her lips. "He said he owes you a large debt. I don't see how that can be given how young you are. But that's what he said."

I shrugged. "He must still have me mistaken for someone else. But if there ever was a debt, I'm sure your inn's fine hospitality has more than repaid it. Thank you again, and until next time." I gave her a parting wave, and she gave me a hesitant smile, returning the wave. Then I gave a few pats to Turtle, who gave me another snort, and I pulled myself to the driver's bench and Charm joined me from the other side. With Turtle's reins in my hands, we set off.

It was only a while afterward that I noticed that Charm was eating bread with a rare expression of satisfaction.

"Where did you get that?"

She eyed me and pointed at the breadbasket between us that had not been there when we arrived at the inn. "That damned kid," I muttered, but I couldn't help but break off a small piece of the fluffy dough and pop into my mouth.

"Mr. Torren's sincerity is wasted on you."

"Better he f-orgets he ever saw me," I said while chewing. "Now, do you remember the directions Tammy gave us last night?"

She replied what might have been a withering look, I wasn't sure, her expression seemed as placid as ever, but she proceeded to describe the way. While we devoured Torren's fresh loaf, we headed down several winding roads before crossing onto the main street of the city, the Elven Pass.

The city looked entirely different during the day, and I found myself smiling as the morning brightened and the street became busy with crowds and wagons and carriages and the sounds of a great city filled the air. Meritas was not as populous as Yestereaster, but it was still the second largest city in the kingdom. Merchants came from across the Visserian continent and the Primordial Sea to trade here, and as we passed markets and squares, I saw many tradesmen haggling and working their wares.

Unlike Yestereaster, which was primarily made of white stone, Meritas was a colorful city composed of dark timber, red brick, and yellow and tan plaster. It'd been a long time since I had visited, and it had grown even more vibrant than I could have hoped for.

I looked over at Charm with a smile to see what she thought of the city's sights, only to find that her expression had not changed from earlier. However, I did notice that her eyes moved from here to there, across the street and off the faces of the people we passed, which I took as a hopeful sign.

We headed down the Elven Pass for nearly half an hour before Charm directed me to make a turn on a smaller street. Then, before long, we had made our way to Sharla's Inn, which had a sign that jutted out from the innhouse prominently displaying its name in wood-scribed letters. The inn was smaller than Tammy's place, but it looked cozy enough. I led Turtle around to the side of the inn, where a stableman was seated, smoking a pipe. He stood up upon seeing us come toward the inn, giving a friendly wave.

"Good morning!" the stableman said, putting a cap on the pipe and tucking it behind his vest. "Staying long?"

"Not sure yet," I replied. "At least a few nights, I figure."

The stableman nodded. "Rest assured, sir, I'll keep good care of your horse and wagon, but if you have any valuables, it's best you take them into the room just in case. We haven't had a thief in some time, but best be safe."

"Oh we don't have much in the way of valuables," I said as I drew my pack from behind my seat and hopped down. "But we'll bring in the sentimental items, as you say."

The man gave me a nod and took the reins of Turtle. I held out my hand for Charm to descend from the wagon, and she took it, as she often did when strangers were present.

"Tell Sharla that you want a room," the stableman said, "and that you've got a wagon. She'll be in the dining room serving breakfast."

"Thank you," I said, and we headed inside. The dining room was conjoined with the small lobby area and there were four benched tables lined up two by two with a few guests seated. I caught sight of the innkeeper as she stepped out of the kitchen with two steaming hot plates. And my eyes lingered.

She was perhaps thirty years of age, and wore a catching dress beneath a tight corset. She had a pretty face and I felt heat rise to my cheeks as she turned and caught my eye. "Oh, welcome," she said with a smile. "You two are in early. Breakfast, a room, or both?"

"Both please, also I was told to inform you we have a wagon–one horse."

"Very good," she said. "It's a shim a night, in-cluding meals and care for your horse and wagon. And I'll need the first night's payment upfront."

"Right, certainly." I dug into my trousers for my coin purse and retrieved two silver coins, placing them in Sharla's outstretched hand.

She held them to her face and turned them in her palm. "My, it's been some time since I've seen first edition shimmers."

"Is that a problem?" I said, suddenly feeling worried. All my coins were age old and I still had a tavern to buy.

Sharla shook her head. "They say the first gen-eration mints hold more silver and gold. Seeing as how they're becoming rarer, if you held onto them for another decade or two, you might just get double for them."

"Oh…" I said "I didn't know. I'm glad you ac-cept them. The bank in Yestereaster gave me only these ones."

"Did they? Must have been a fella that didn't know better and wanted to get rid of them.

They're worth ten percent more at the currency desks if you'd like to go trade them. I can watch your wagon in the meantime if you'd like."

"Ah, no that's alright," I said, and noting that all the tinkers and traders we had passed on our journey had not mentioned this difference in value. "We've only been in the city for a night and are still quite tired from our trip. Perhaps we'll do some trading later after we've settled in."

"Very good," Sharla said again. "Let me get you two some breakfast, then."

"Forgive my intrusion," Charm said. "The innkeeper of the Happy Crow asked us to inform you that she sent us over to you."

"Oh, you stayed with Tammy did you?" Sharla said. "How's she and Torren doing?"

"Well," I said. "We enjoyed her soups and good cheer."

"A friend of Tammy's is a friend of mine. Let me give you our corner room. It's right next to the latrine and away from the street so you can get a good night's rest." Sharla looked at the coins in her hand again. "And I'll take a shim off your stay, if you stay three nights." She winked at me, which sent my heart pounding harder than catching a demon lord's lance. "Let me get you started with breakfast. Be back in a spell."

"She seems nice," I said to Charm, who gave me another one of her flat, unreadable looks.

We took our seats across from each other at the empty table in the room.

"This is a fine inn," I said as I looked around the room. "Maybe we'll be able to find a place as nice as this."

What I got in reply was another arch in Charm's brow.

"What?" I said.

"You seem awfully cheerful."

"So what if I am?" I said, crossing my arms. "What's wrong with that?"

"Nothing. Only I did not realize an innkeeper's cleavage could so easily raise your spirits."

"It rose nothing! And keep your voice down!"

"You are the one shouting," Charm said in her monotone voice.

I looked around and noticed some of the breakfasters had turned to see what the commotion was. I slouched down in my seat. "I'm just enjoying the city, that's all."

"I am glad to hear it," Charm said. "For a moment I was worried I was traveling with a teenage pervert who upon sealing his immortal gates had also unsealed all of his uncontrolled bodily urges."

"Will you keep quiet! Someone might hear you!"

This time I hissed it, but I had still been louder than Charm. She made this point by arching her brow again.

"Look, nothing's been unsealed, alright? It's just going to take some time to get used to... things. Don't tell me you haven't experienced anything new."

Charm touched one of the strands of pink hair on her shoulders and rubbed it between her fingers. "I have no such issues. Only a fool would allow their mind to be ruled by their body."

"Here are your eggs, sausage, and toast," Sharla said as she appeared at our table, leaning over to serve our plates and utensils. Suddenly my heart was thumping again and I had to tear my eyes away, landing my gaze hard on my plate. I barely noticed her leaving our table.

"Idiot," Charm mumbled, shaking her head as she took a bite of her eggs.

"What was that?" I said, looking up at Charm, my voice taking on a tinge of offense.

"I said 'itiut,'" Charm said, "It is a word from a foreign language that has long been lost to time."

"Really?" I said with my own flattened gaze. "And what does the word 'itiut' mean?"

"Hmm... There is no direct equivalent in contemporary Vissish. But loosely translated, it means 'an imbecile that lacks basic intelligence or mental functionality.' In simpler terms, an idiot."

"Then why didn't you just say idiot!?"

"I assumed your lust-riddled brain would lack the attention span to ask me for the translation and thus my insult would be successfully completed without notice."

My breath choked in my mouth as a thousand thoughts and emotions swirled in me. I rested my clenched fists down onto the tabletop. "How is it possible that this explanation of your simplistic insult has resulted in a far longer and expanded offense!?"

Charm shrugged, "Given my current circumstances, I have little choice but to obey you and answer your extremely stupit questions."

I pointed my fork at her, "Don't even start with that 'stupit' nonsense! You're clearly making these words up."

"Did I say stupit?" Charm said looking up. "My apologies, I must have lapsed into the ancient tongue again. However I assure you the language is real. Would you like me to explain the meaning of the word 'stupit'? Or has your attention already been lost on another set of exemplary breasts?"

"My attention hasn't been lost on anything! I'm listening just fine, so go ahead and explain away! No wait! Don't explain! This is an elaborate trap! Please can we just stop this conversation?"

Charm shrugged and gently sank her fork into a sausage link. "As you please."

I watched her carefully. I could not remember us speaking for so long, especially about trivial matters. And despite the empty contents of our words, I wondered if this was her way of enjoying herself. But her face revealed nothing. It was as emotionally flat as ever, and I could not discern her feelings. She had kept it like this since our journey began.

I sighed heavily and forked a slice of fried egg. We had a busy day ahead and my stomach was growling. But before the whites could make their way to my mouth, someone had pulled a chair to our table and joined us. I turned to our new table mate with surprise, my mouth still open and readied to receive a bite of eggs. But the man's face gave me pause. A white mask covered his eyes, revealing only his mouth, which smiled with clean white teeth. He wore a shimmering dark green cloak over a leather vest held together by bright gold buttons.

"My name is Harkness. It is a pleasure to meet you."

# CHAPTER 5: SERVICES

I stared at the masked man with my brows raised and my mouth hung open and my fork-struck eggs paused just below my chin. Somehow this Harkness character had found me, but more importantly, he wore *a mask*. It was all white and glittering, the two eye holes covered by opaque white crystals.

*Can he even see out of that thing?* I wondered. *And why is he wearing it in broad daylight?* Maybe his eyes were injured and the upper part of his face is deformed. But the man definitely could see, given the way he moved.

"Do not be frightened," Harkness continued after the long pause in which I had not lowered my eggs or closed my jaw. "I'm here to offer my services, of which there are many, and to meet you."

I continued to gape at him, and my eye began twitching, my lips were quivering, and my whole body shook. The eggs slipped off my fork and fell back on my plate.

"Quit your mockery!" Sard had stepped forward with a snarl on his face and a finger jabbed in my direction. "We know you aren't scared."

"Please don't be mad." I stopped shaking and wiped my mouth with a napkin. "I don't want to offend anyone this time, I know Sardy doesn't like it when people aren't shivering around him."

"I'll give you something to be afraid of!" Sard took a step forward and somehow froze his off-balance body mid launch upon seeing Harkness' raised hand.

"I told him there was no need to fear, Sard. Are you going against my wishes?"

Sard bowed low immediately. "I would never dare. Forgive me, Harkness."

Harkness waved his hand lazily. "All is well," he said without looking back at his man. He smiled back at me. "Where were we? That's it, my esteemed services had just been generously offered. But a thought has come to me, and I'd like to ask you a question first. Tell me, where in the hierarchy do you belong?"

"Uhh... I beg your pardon?"

"Where in the hierarchy do you belong? I see that you are dressed as a simple commoner, but you have an unusual bearing, and your manner suggests a higher station in the hierarchy."

"What hierarchy?"

"The only one that matters. The hierarchy of society."

"I guess I fall somewhere..."

"Where?"

"Oh you know, near the bottom but not far from the top."

Harkness' grin widened. "How can I be of service to you?"

"Erm… actually, I don't need any service, I don't think," I snuck a glance at Charm and whispered under my breath, "Do we need any service?"

Charm, who had mostly ignored us until now, shook her head and sipped tea from her mug.

"Everyone needs something," Harkness said, undeterred. "Say, for instance, an introduction to the many distinguished landlords in this city looking to sell their inns and taverns. Which wards are you interested in?"

"Well… we've just arrived and haven't seen the city much yet, but Angelmore and Lumitra seemed nice."

Harkness slapped his leg with a grin. His mannerisms almost made you forget he was wearing a mask. "Then you'll be in need of my service indeed for you must be part of the aristocracy or at least a close friend of the court to own a pristine establishment in one of those wards. And that does not yet account for the cost. At least several hundred gold brilliances will be necessary, which I could, loan to a man like you."

I wasn't quite sure if several hundred gold brilliances was still a fortune given the depreciation of gold over the past hundred years, but I was sure it was a lot. "You would lend me such a sum without even knowing me?"

"I do know you," Harkness said, "I have a good eye for people, and I can tell you're special."

I dropped my face into my hands. "Not again. My ungodly good looks are causing another scene."

"Come come, there's no need to play coy," Harkness said. "A man who can make Torren bow and frighten Sard is certainly a man I wish to befriend."

"I wasn't frightened," Sard put in.

Harkness snapped his head to his subordinate. He spoke no words but the smile was gone from his masked face and it felt as if the room had turned cold. Sard's features changed from anger to shame and he bowed once more, moving away slowly, step by step until he turned and exited the doorway of the inn.

Harkness turned back to me with the smile as if it had never left. "So what do you say? Will you take my offer?"

I noticed the look Charm gave me now which I took to mean how I handled this moment would determine just how much danger we were in.

"I do apologize," I said, "but I don't see how a misunderstanding with an old man and the fact I didn't bow down to a bully somehow makes me worthy of credit. We're looking to set up shop in your city and gain the opportunities it has to offer, no different than any other of the common folk entering the city gates today."

"Common folk, you say?" Harkness said with that perfect smile. "I've known Torren since he arrived in Meritas. He is a proud man with high honor. His family borrowed from me to fix up their inn, and they still owe me a sizable sum. But he would not bow to me nor any man, and certainly to no common lad if he were truly common. I've asked around about your entry into Meritas. From Yestereaster, the gate guards said you claimed. Those routes have been harassed by bandits since early spring. Only armed caravans have been getting through unscathed. Then there is the fact you intend to purchase a tavern. Even in the poorer wards, it'll cost a bright coin, for land ownership offers immediate citizenship in Meritas, and I assume you did not arrive with an empty purse, though I do wonder about the source of your funds and their purity."

"Now wait just a minute!" I exclaimed. "Just who are you to question the authority of my coin? My father runs a legitimate business, far bigger and more legitimate than yours, that's for certain." I glared at him for a long moment, then blinked as if suddenly conscious of my words. "Look, I'd prefer not to explain myself, other than to say a man needs to make his own way. Sure, my family might have fronted me some small funds, but they never compensated me for all the trips and contributions I made since I was a boy. So we're even as far as I'm concerned."

"I see, then Torren knows your family. They must have done him some great favor."

"Huh?" I said. "Never met the man, that was just some mistake."

Harkness watched me for a long moment but I could not see his eyes past the crystal eyes of his mask. He slapped the table suddenly, loud and hard. "Well then, I won't delay your business any further. If I can be of any service, please do let me know. You can reach me by leaving word at any inn in the city." He bowed to Charm. "My Lady."

Charm eyed me after Harkness took his leave. "So... you intended to give him the impression that you belong to a merchant family of Yestereaster."

"What do you mean 'intended'? That is the impression I gave."

Charm arched a brow at me.

"What?" I said.

"You did not react when he hit the table," Charm said.

"So?" I said, but before she responded, I had already begun to recognize my error. "Oh... crap."

Charm nodded. The issue wasn't that he had hit the table hard, it was the way he had done it. His hand had come high and moved toward me first before it swung down against the table. Any normal man would have flinched, or put up a blocking hand, or moved out of their seat, or at least blinked. It had been a test, and I was certain Harkness' interest in me had only grown.

Sharla returned to refill our cups of tea. "It's not any of my business," she said as she poured the hot orange liquid into my mug. "But it's best not to get involved with that man if you know what's good for you. And that's saying it sweetly."

"We've been warned," I said. "Don't tell me he has something on you too."

Sharla smiled at me and I felt my pulse. "Not me, but plenty of business owners in the city. They say Harkness cares less about coin and more about owning people. I'd rather lose my inn than be a slave to a man like that."

"I hear you," I said, casting a nervous glance at Charm before turning back to Sharla. "Say, would you know of any properties in the area that are available for sale?"

"As a matter of fact, I do. It's not in this ward but just down the way, Maeve is selling her inn. Large space though, what kind of place are you looking for?"

"Some place with heart and character, and enough room for me to build a brewery."

Sharla shrugged. "Worth a look then, I'd say. The inn's right on the main road of Southbank, with south-facing windows and a large common area. I'll point you in the right direction when you're ready to head out."

"Appreciate it," I said with a smile. She smiled back and left us.

I watched her go and said, "This is going to be no easy task, Charm."

"What terrible plan is the pervert concocting?"

"I'm not a pervert, nothing wrong with admiring a beautiful woman. And I was talking about buying a tavern!"

"If we restrict ourselves to the commoner's wards of the city, I see no issue, not with your funds."

"Hmph, your lack of experience living as a simpleton shows in this matter, Charm," I said. "Purchasing property is no easy thing. There are no guarantees. The atmosphere has to be right, the location has to be right, and most important of all, the layout of the tavern has to be right. We'll need to pour over city maps to find areas worthy of our time. Then there is the issue of the seller. Perhaps the tavern is already spoken for, and they have brought us in at the last moment to gouge the first buyer for some additional coin. Perhaps there will be a bidding war, of which we will of course win, but that takes time, and while we are bidding, a better property elsewhere might emerge, splitting our hearts and resolve. And all that doesn't even include the condition of the tavern. Some place might look nice and inviting, but for all we know the proprietor's trying to rid their hands of a sewer-clogged heap of brittle crap that'll fall apart in a year or two."

Charm looked unperturbed.

"I'm just saying, this is likely going to be a long drawn-out process, and we need to be prepared for that."

"I think I understand."

"Do you?"

Charm nodded. "The pervert wishes to stay at this inn longer for the pretty innkeeper."

"That's not what I said at all!" I glared at her, then looked over toward the kitchen to make sure Sharla hadn't overheard.

I leaned toward Charm. "I'm just saying that we gotta get it right. We gotta see what's out there before making any final decisions."

"Then, let us begin," Charm said.

# CHAPTER 6: THROWN DAGGERS

"This is the place we're buying!"

Charm gave me one of her deadpan looks. "This is likely not the place Sharla was referring to."

"Sure it is! We're in Southbank, on The Cobblestone Road, and I don't see another building big enough to be an inn."

"The description does not match. It looks expensive."

She was right. The place had white marble walls and a beautifully ornamented smooth timber door. It was better than any place I could have imagined. As nice as any of the buildings we had passed in Angelmore, so much so that it stood out in this neighborhood, which wasn't poor by any means. The cobblestones on the aptly named road looked to be as old as the sky, but they were well-maintained. The other buildings on the street, most of which were shops and small cafes, were colorful, clean, and well-kept. The ward was nothing like any of the others I'd seen so far. Southbank was colorful and cozy.

"Let's go speak to the owner and get this deal signed."

Charm shook her head but made no verbal protest and followed me inside. The interior was even more beautiful than the exterior. But the bar area was a little small, and many small tables covered with pristine white tablecloths were arranged in neat, evenly spaced rows across the main floor. But that wasn't a problem. I could change all that.

"Barkeep!" I said cheerfully to the man in the silk shirt behind the counter. "We're here to see the owner."

The man turned with a frown that only deepened after giving us a once over. "I am the owner, and there are no barkeeps in this establishment."

"It's wonderful to meet you! I hear you've listed your property for sale, and I would like to buy it!"

The man laughed. "Boy, you couldn't afford it."

"Name your price," I said and noted Charm was shaking her head again.

The owner shrugged. "Five hundred gold brilliances."

It was more than I expected, as much as Harkness said it would cost to buy a place in Angelmore.

"Hmm," I said, scratching my chin. "You have a deal, but I would need your secrecy in the matter. Although we would have to register it with the local officials... But I guess that's just a risk we'll have to take."

The owner's grin vanished. "Get out of here, I'm in no mood for hooligans today."

"I am serious about my offer."

"Sure you are, and I'm the Count of Mapleber-
ry. Get out-"

"But Maeve, you won't find a better deal. I can
pay you today."

"My name isn't Maeve, you fool. Now get out
before I call the ward guards!"

He shooed us out and slammed the door shut in
our faces.

"That wasn't Maeve?" I said to Charm.

"Maeve is traditionally a woman's name, to my
understanding."

Only now did I notice the sign that named the
place. "The Grand Taphouse... hmm... Sharla did
say it was supposed to be an inn."

"It appears you did not properly lead Turtle
according to her directions," Charm said as she
wandered off.

"Where are you going?" I said, walking after
her.

"To get directions from a shopkeeper whose ap-
pearance isn't so distracting to cause the loss of
hearing.

"I wasn't distracted!"

***

"This is the place?" I said, feeling disappointed. Charm nodded. Once again we were standing in front of a building, but this one lacked all the splendor of the Grand Taphouse. In fact, if put side by side, this building looked like a dump. However, it was certainly an inn with two stories, several sets of windows taking in the southern sunlight, and two doors facing The Cobblestone Road. One of the windows had a sign placed in the frame with the words "For Sale."

The inn was framed by dark timber that crisscrossed against yellow plaster, and a band of brick wrapped around the base of the inn. Unlike many other buildings on the street, this one stood farther apart from its neighbors, which I found unusual. But there wasn't anything particularly wrong with the place, it just wasn't the marbled mansion down the street.

"Shall we go inside?" Charm said, arching a brow at me.

"I guess so," I said, though I already had a feeling I wasn't going to like the place.

We stepped through the door that was part of the smaller section of the inn that protruded toward the road. It led into what looked like a lobby area, a space large enough to be a tavern all on its own. However, it was entirely empty save for the key counter at the very end of the room.

"Hello?" I said. "Anyone home?"

The inn creaked as if in reply, but there was no human response. I eyed the dark wood that covered the floor and ceilings. It was better constructed than I had thought. Nothing flashy, but plenty solid.

We took a left turn down an open hallway at the end of the lobby. There was a door on each side and the entryway to the main hall at the end. One door led to a spacious kitchen and the other to an equally spacious storage room. Both were nearly empty like the lobby, however the kitchen had two plates set on a drying rack.

Charm and I continued down the corridor and into the main hall. It was perhaps three times larger than the lobby and far larger than what I had expected looking from the outside. The second-floor was left open and the ceiling was seven man-heights high. A staircase led to a mezzanine where I assumed the rooms were. The place was so big I couldn't imagine what I'd do with it all if I were to buy the place. But I could not deny its beauty. Morning light fell through the second floor windows and warmed the entire space.

Then I heard footsteps and a young man with hair the color of straw came down the stairs. He was carrying a stack of drawers that may have belonged to several nightstands.

"Oh, hello there," he said, peeking past the stack as he descended the stairs. "Are you two looking for rooms?"

I pointed toward the sign that was blocking one of the windows. "I thought the place was for sale."

"Ah yes, but before you go, you should know we're offering severe discounts for any travelers... hold on a minute," he came to a stop on the very last stair and raised his head above the stack of drawers and eyebrows seemed to raise even higher. "Are you two interested in buying the inn?"

"We may be," I said. "We were hoping for a tour."

"Of course!" the young man said and dropped the stack of drawers beside the staircase as if they were suddenly rubbish. "Right away, please follow me." He turned and headed back up the staircase, then paused and turned around. "Ah, perhaps I should introduce the dining hall since we are already here. It is the best part of the inn, certainly."

"No need, we've seen it," I said. "And the lobby too," I added when he pointed down the corridor we had come from.

"Of course, to the second floor then!" the young man headed up the stairs again, then paused. "Pardon, I haven't even introduced myself," he said, chuckling nervously. "I'm Albert, the inn is owned by my grandmother. She should be here any moment, and I'm sure she'd love to speak with you."

"I'm Arch," I said. "And this is Charm."

Charm's brow twitched at me at the mention of her name, but she gave a slight bow to Albert, who returned it right away. The whole thing was made extra awkward by the fact we were on the stairs. Albert turned again and led us up to the second floor. We walked beside the railing and made a horseshoe shaped turn around to a hall with several doors on each side. I realized we were standing above the lobby area.

"Here are the rooms," Albert said. "We have less than your average inn, but our rooms are plenty comfortable." He opened the nearest door and led us into a square room with a single cot. It was large enough to fit another bed or a desk, but there was no furniture in the room save for the bed and a nightstand, which had missing drawers.

"Why have you removed the drawers?" I said.

Albert's nervous chuckle came again. "Well, we figured the new owners would want to install their own furniture. But we've left the beds in each of the rooms. They're mighty fine mattresses."

"And the locks?" Charm said to both our surprise.

I looked down to find the door's keyhole and sure enough, the locking mechanism had been removed entirely, leaving an open gap.

"Ah... uh..." Albert said uncertainly, scratching at the back of his straw-colored hair. "You'd want your own keys, of course. That's right, you wouldn't want anyone else to have the keys. You'd need them all changed, so we removed them for you."

Charm turned her eyes to me and raised a brow. She was right, there was definitely something fishy going on. Albert seemed to notice our nonverbal exchange and he quickly said, "There's also the cellar I've yet to introduce. Please come with me!"

We followed Albert back down the stairs to a door beside the staircase that descended down another flight of stairs. Looking back, if I had to name the moment that it changed for me, it was likely then. The cellar was nearly as large as the tavern's entire first floor, and the walls were made of warm-hued brick.

"We don't use this space much other than for storage. But as you can see, the foundation is plenty strong. Say, do you have an inn that you intend to move here?"

"No," I said. "We're opening a tavern."

"Oh... a tavern..." Albert said uncertainly, likely thinking the same faults I had noted earlier. But those had seemingly disappeared from my mind.

"That's right," I said. "A tavern that brews its own ales with the finest equipment known to man. Equipment that'll need plenty of space and be kept safe and dry."

"Oh," Albert said, his eyes lighting up. "Then this is the perfect place for you, then, certainly."

"Why are you selling the inn?" Charm said, once again to both our surprise. We seemed to have forgotten she was with us.

"A fair question, indeed," Albert said, the nervousness returning to his features, then they seemed to relax. "My grandmother was once an adventurer. She opened this inn to take care of me... but now that I have come of age, there's no reason for her to run it any more." Albert smiled softly. "She was an excellent innkeeper, but she's always been an adventurer at heart. We intend to go on a journey to see the northern tip of Visseria after the inn is sold. Maybe we'll reach it, maybe we'll settle somewhere else on the way."

I nodded along. Charm said nothing. But Albert didn't seem to notice us. The nervousness crept back into his features.

"And... and we've had trouble running it. Southbank has become a popular ward, but there's plenty of inns all around. We don't have many rooms for the space we have, and there is some fair competition in the area. That and... we have debts, which makes it hard for us to keep up with renovations and our offerings." Albert let out a sigh, but he seemed relieved to have said it all.

"You sold the locks to pay your debts?" Charm said.

"Ah... yes." Albert looked down. "We had to close down, just last week in fact, not that we'd turn anyone away looking to spend a night. We've stayed open for as long as we could. But I'm sure you two will do better. It's an excellent space for a tavern. And if you're brewing your own ales, you'll certainly be unique in Southbank."

"It's a fine space," I said. "We've just begun looking around, but we're interested. We're staying at Sharla's Inn. Don't sell the place without letting us know."

Albert looked up and a hopeful smile sprang up on his face. "Certainly, Mr. Arch, certainly. I'm sure my grandmother would love to speak with you and answer any questions you might have. She knows all about the history of the inn and Southbank. I'm sure-"

A door opened and footsteps could be heard upstairs.

"Oh! I think that's her returning from the market. Come, let me introduce you."

We followed Albert back up the stairs to the main hall. Sure enough, someone had entered the inn, but it wasn't Albert's grandmother. It was a large man, tall, with a sharp face and sharper eyes.

He stared into me with a gaze like thrown daggers.

# CHAPTER 7: LOANS AND DISCOUNTS

Another man entered behind Sard as we conducted our staring contest. He was a short, older man, wearing robes that looked like the kind that might belong to some kind of official position. His head was partially bald, and the eyes behind his wireframe spectacles were shrewd if bored.

"Oh, Mr. Sard," Albert said awkwardly, rubbing the back of his head. "I didn't think you would come so early..." Albert gave an uncomfortable glance to Charm and me as if he was uncertain of how to explain the situation.

He didn't really need to. I guessed from the way the inn had been emptied and Harkness' method of business that Albert and his grandmother had taken a loan from the partial crime boss. Apparently, today was payment day.

"Where's Maeve?" Sard said without taking his eyes off of me.

"She's out at the market. She'll be back soon... I think. Perhaps if you came back later..."

"No." Sard finally drew his eyes to the young man. "I'll wait."

Albert's eyes dropped to his feet, then he looked at Charm and I again. He appeared to be in a tight pickle. "It's still an hour before noon bell," Albert said. "I wish I had something to serve you while you waited. Maybe you'd prefer to wait at one of the cafes down the street. I can come get you when my grand-"

"No," Sard said again, just as curtly as the first time. Then he walked to the nearest wall and leaned against it with his arms crossed, his eyes returning to examine me.

"I beg your pardon," the older man said now as he took out a handkerchief to wipe some sweat from his forehead. "If the proprietor isn't here yet, I would not mind waiting at a cafe. Is there one conveniently close by?"

I glanced at him. I was pretty sure I figured out the relationship between Albert and Sard, but I had no idea where to place the older gentleman.

"Yes, sir," Albert said. "The Lucky Bean is just down the street. You could also try the Grand-"

"I'm not waiting on you, old man," Sard growled. "If Maeve wants to drag her feet, it'll be her fault if she runs out of time, not ours. This is getting done today."

The older man sighed and tucked his handkerchief into the folds of his robes. "So be it. Let us hope she arrives soon, or you'll soon find this notary sitting on the floor."

Albert paled at the old man's remark. "You are a notary?"

"Indeed, I am a notary of the Meritan Magistrate. Since your loan payment has been missed and extended three times already, your lender has requested my presence. If you are unable to pay today, your lender is within his rights to take ownership of your properties. Of course, he will have to remunerate you if the property's value exceeds what you still owe."

"It far exceeds what we owe!" Albert exclaimed. "You can't let him do this!"

The notary shrugged. "I am an impartial witness. If the interest due on your debt is paid, there will be no possession of your property."

"This was your plan all along," Albert said, shooting Sard a hateful look. I was surprised to see it on the mild-mannered boy.

Sard chuckled. "We gave you a fair deal. The fairest deal we give, with a capped rate, which is why we had it ratified by the magistrate. It's not my fault you haven't paid up. We've got to recoup our costs one way or another."

"But we just need more time," Albert said. "We'll find a buyer any moment, and we'll pay out our debt in full."

"You heard the notary. We'll pay you the difference." Sard grinned. "But it'll be up to the ward's business bureau to decide what fair value this place holds. Then again, the appraisal might come in lower than what you owe given the defective foundation of this inn and its fragile structure. Then you'll be the one owing us the difference."

Albert's face burned red with anger. "You know there's no problem with the foundation!"

Sard shrugged. "I beg to differ. We'll let the experts decide when the time comes."

"The experts in your pocket!" Albert turned to the notary again. "Please, you mustn't let him do this. You heard his intentions. This inn is all we have left."

The notary sighed and removed his thin spectacles, rubbing the glass with the sleeve of his robes. "I am an impartial witness of the Meritan Magistrate," he repeated. "The details of your loan and the appraisal process is managed by your local business bureau. I have no say in the matter."

Albert was pale and wide eyed. Sard smirked and stared up at the sky through the window. "Noon is not far now, best pay up soon, if you have the funds."

Then we all turned to the sound of the main hall's door swinging open and a bag of coins landing loudly at Sard's feet.

"Grandmother!" Albert called hopefully to the figure standing in the doorway.

She was a tall woman despite her age. White hair framed a strong jaw. Her shoulders were wide and I could tell by her bearing that she had once been a warrior. She stared at Sard with cold eyes.

Sard picked up the sack and peered inside, a grin spreading on his face. "If this were a bag of silver, Maeve, it might have been enough."

"You'll get the rest by tonight," Maeve said.

Sard shook his head. "The contract is up by noon bell. Your inn belongs to Harkness now. If you sign the title over without trouble, I'll guarantee you won't owe us anything further. Otherwise we'll take you to court for our missing payments, and we'll let the appraisers judge the tavern's value."

"You won't take my inn," Maeve said with steel in her voice.

"Yes I will."

"Not while my heart's still beating."

The words surprised me, as the old woman had said them plainly and yet each syllable held the strength of truth.

Sard smiled as if he was fine by that, but he said, "Don't make this more difficult than it needs to be. The place never stood a chance. It's cursed land. Best we take it over instead of some other unlucky businessman. Harkness intends to keep the property."

"For what purpose?" Maeve said. "Is it for the new don that's been vying for Urindal's power? What does this new don want with all the properties he's been snatching up? What's he storing, Sard?"

Sard frowned and his eyes narrowed. "Careful now. Don't be saying things that aren't any of your business. Harkness doesn't work for anyone and he doesn't go against anyone. He's a friend to all."

"Pardon me," I said with a cough. I was uninterested in all the underworld politics, but they'd mentioned one thing that had piqued my interest. All eyes turned to me. It seemed everyone had forgotten that Charm and I were still there. "You, uh, mentioned this land was cursed?"

"Foolish superstition," Maeve said as she looked me over with some curiosity.

Sard grinned. "It used to be an empty lot for a reason. Legend has it that this was where they did the beheadings when Meritas was still a village."

"None of that matters," Maeve said. "Superintendent Tallow built this building to make a happy establishment for the ward. I promised him to make it a place of joy. And I aim to keep that promise even if I can't do it myself. If he were still in charge, he'd never let gangsters have any part of it."

"Harkness is no gangster. All his business is all above board. You know this, Maeve. Don't attack the reputation of my employer when you are the one who has broken…"

The argument between Sard and Maeve continued but faded from my mind as I looked over the dark wood beams and the cracked plaster walls and red brick foundation peeking past the floorboards along the walls. I wondered what about this place was so valuable that Maeve would risk her life for it. It didn't have any of the splendor of the Grand Taphouse. It was true there was plenty of space, and the natural light made everything feel warm and pleasant, though this mattered little for a tavern that mainly operated at night. But as I glanced around, I felt as if I could see it being filled with patrons, perhaps even more so than I could of the Grand Taphouse. Unlike marble, there was a certain comfortable warmth about the timber beams and yellowed plaster. Like the kind of place you'd go after a long day, still wearing your work uniform. A place you could just sit back and relax and sip on a freshly brewed ale…

"I'd like to buy the place," I said before I really knew what I was saying. But once the words had exited my mouth, I knew them to be true.

The hall had gone quiet and once again I had captured everyone's attention. Even Charm looked surprised.

"That's wonderful," Albert said, a look of great relief on his features.

"What's your asking price?" I said to Maeve.

"What's your business?" she said, giving me a closer inspection now that I was a potential buyer.

"I'm looking to open a tavern. Not an inn, sorry, but I do think this place could work as a tavern with some effort."

"It's too large for a tavern," Maeve said.

"Grandmother!" Albert protested, apparently worried they were going to lose their only prospective buyer.

But Maeve was right. The place was big, and a tavern, especially a new tavern, would feel empty with such a big space.

"Perhaps..." Maeve said. "If you began by opening the lobby only, and if you grew enough, you could then open the main hall one day."

"That's not a bad idea, actually," I said, rubbing my chin.

"Why do you wish to open a tavern?" Maeve said.

"I intend to brew my own ales and-"

"Enough of this!" Sard growled. "Your debt has not been paid. The inn is mine."

"We have until noon!" Albert insisted. "We can get the transfer papers signed now with Mr. Arch."

"The business bureau is closed today," Sard said, grinning. "You wouldn't be able to make the transfer until tomorrow. Meanwhile my debt is due now."

Albert's face dropped, all the hope spilling out of him. Maeve's jaw clenched.

"What's your asking price?" I said.

She blinked at me. Then she said with a hint of hope in her voice, "I'd ask for a hundred and fifty gold brilliances."

"I can do that," I said, nodding.

Sard scowled at our continued conversation. He glared at Maeve. "If you won't hand me your deed, then the notary will sign your failure to pay. Your deed will be forfeit, and you will have no power to sell what you no longer possess."

"You must give us more time," Albert said to the notary. "We have a buyer ready!"

The notary sighed and shrugged. "The due date is the due date. If the owed interest is not paid today, the lender is entitled to take possession of your property to recoup the full amount of the loan just as you are entitled to receive the payment of the difference in value as required by law."

"How much do you owe on the loan?" I said to Maeve, ignoring everyone else.

"Forty-two gold brilliances in total, including our missed interest payments."

I nodded to Charm and she withdrew a pouch from her travel sack. She counted out forty-two gold brilliances, wrapped them in a thin leather

binding, and handed them to Maeve. The old adventurer looked at me with unbridled surprise.

I smiled back at her. "I expect a forty-two bril-
lance discount on your asking price."

# CHAPTER 8: FORCED HANDS

Maeve's stare of disbelief lasted only two moments. She nodded to me once, then took the leather-wrapped coins and handed them to the notary. "The sun has not yet set. Take account that my payment has been made in full."

The notary took the wrapping and counted the coins once more. Then he handed them to Sard, whose scowl looked to be chiseled from stone.

"Your debt has been repaid," the notary said in the same matter-of-fact voice as before.

Sard backhanded the leather parcel from the notary's grasp, sending the parcel flying and coins scattering across the floorboards. "That's not her coin."

The notary stared down at the scattered coins and sighed once more. "There is no law that forbids a man to give away his wealth in Meritas."

"May I consider this matter resolved in the eyes of the magistrate?" Maeve said.

The notary nodded. "You may. The payment has been offered. If the lender does not wish to accept, that is his choice."

Sard cursed and knelt down beside the fallen coins, scooping them back into parcel and tucked it away into the back of his belt. Then he turned his darkened eyes to me. "I won't forget this."

I nodded. "I am glad your mind is capable of storing memories."

Sard grinned wide. "Think you're funny, do you?" In an instant the smile was gone and he had launched across the room, his hand clutched around my neck, slamming my back into the rear wall.

Albert let out a cry of horror, followed by gasps from the others.

"You've chosen the wrong man to meddle with," Sard hissed.

I began to choke under his grip. I grabbed onto his wrist with my left hand and his hand on my throat with my right.

"Let him go at once!" Maeve bellowed.

Even the notary no longer looked impartial. "Sir, you must stop this violence!"

Charm looked unmoved, though there was an arch in her brow. In reply, I convulsed harder, saliva drooling from my mouth.

Sard grinned at my gurgling face, satisfied that his point had been made and a lesson taught. Then he released the pressure on my neck.

Or at least he tried to.

But his hand didn't leave my neck. His look of satisfaction was replaced by a frown of confusion. "What-"

"H-el-p!" I gasped. "I ca-n-ot br-ea-"

My right hand held his fingers firm against my throat, preventing him from releasing his hold. And with my left hand, I tightened my grip around his wrist, until the little bones in his wrist cracked beneath my pressure.

The big man screamed out in pain, lifting me off the wall and slamming me against the floor.

"Call the ward guard!" Maeve shouted to Albert as she launched herself around Sard's arm. The notary was soon on him too, pulling back against Sard's fingers. I released my grip on the one finger the notary got a hold of, but held the rest of his fingers tight against my throat. Then I writhed against the ground, my eyes rolling back as if all life was being choked out of me.

"Let him go! Have you gone mad!?" the notary screamed, all the matter-of-factness gone from his voice.

Sard caught his breath, and seemed ready to answer, but then I tightened my grip on his wrist once more, crumbling bone into tendon, and he let out another howl of agony, sliding me back and forth against the floor.

Slowly, carefully, I made a show of pushing his hand away from mine as if with great difficulty, the others aiding me, although they were in fact pushing against my strength and not his. Finally, I let go of my hold on Sard's arm, releasing the tension, and we all fell away from each other, landing in a close circle.

I coughed heavily, gasping for air. "H-e tried to kill me."

"Madman." The notary shook his head in half disbelief, while mumbling to himself. "I knew Harkness' reputation, but to think his people would try to kill a man in front of so many witnesses..."

"Don't you try anything!" Maeve said, pointing a finger at Sard. "The ward guard will be here any moment, murderer!"

Sard was gripping his wounded wrist. But at this, he looked up. "I'm not the one–he did this!" Sard said, gesturing to me.

"J-ust because I p-aid for her loan?" I exclaimed hoarsely. "What kind of logic is that!?"

"No! You forced my hand!"

"That is no excuse for attempted murder!" Maeve shouted back.

"That's not what I mean!" Sard cried out with agony almost as great as when I'd grinded his wrist.

Maeve raised her fists, readying herself for a fight. "The ward guard will be here any moment, I'll take you on until they do."

Sard hissed a curse and shot a look of pure death at me, then he turned and ran out the door.

I watched him go and let out a deep breath, falling back against the ground. The notary let out his own breath and wobbled over to check on me. "Are you alright boy? I was certain he had already crushed your windpipe."

"If it wasn't for you and Maeve, he would have," I said, rubbing at my neck.

Charm gave me a flat, unimpressed gaze. She knew I was fine.

A moment later, Albert arrived with several ward guards in tow. "Captain Kainlin of the Ward Guard is here!" Albert shouted as he entered the room, likely intending to frighten Sard if he were still here.

"He's already gone," Maeve said to the man wearing the captain's insignia on his plate armor.

"What exactly happened here?" Kainlin said, surveying us with wide eyes.

"It was Harkness' man, Sard," the notary said. "I was called here to conduct a routine loan repayment. The young man here paid Maeve's loan and the brute went into a rage. He let out screams of fury as he tried to kill the boy before our own very eyes. I've never seen anything so barbaric in all my days."

The captain looked dumbfounded. "Harkness' man? I can't believe Harkness would allow such a thing."

"You didn't see it," Maeve said. "He attacked Mr. Gustkin and threw him against the wall, then against the ground, screaming as if trying to choke him with everything he had."

"Is this true?" the guard said to the notary.

The notary nodded. "It is. I would not believe it if I had not witnessed it myself. To think such a thing would happen in the good ward of South-bank. The man had gone mad. Absolutely mad."

The captain still seemed unable to believe what he was hearing. Or maybe he didn't want to. It seemed Harkness' reach even extended into this ward's officials.

"It was terrible," said a female voice. And to my shock, Charm was wiping something from her cheek, her bangs covered her eyes. She turned away when we all looked at her.

"It was as if he had been possessed by a demon," she said quietly, "as if he had lost all control. And the way his veins were popping everywhere. He seemed a rabid animal lashing out without thought, no longer human."

"Good Celeru," Kainlin said more to himself than anyone else. "The man must have been on some kind of medicament. I-I... I'll have to issue a warrant for his arrest. Who knows who else he'll attack?" He looked up at me. "Do you need the healer's ward, boy?"

I rubbed at my neck and shook my head. "I think I'll be okay," I said.

Kainlin nodded. "Where are you staying?"

"Sharla's Inn in Keeper's Garden," Charm said. "But Harkness knows we are there."

"Best you find new lodging then," Kainlin said. "I'll post two of my men here tonight."

"You could stay here," Maeve said to me. But Charm gave me a look to say that she did not want to stay in a place that had been emptied of furnishings. Somehow, in that look, I knew she expected me to honor her wishes in return for playing along with my ruse.

"We couldn't trouble you or put you in danger," I said. "Are there any other inns nearby?"

"You could stay at the Black Moon Inn," Maeve said. "Expensive, but you'll be safe there. It's just down the street and around the corner."

"Sounds good to me," I said.

Maeve came to me and held out her hand. "Thank you," she said, "for everything."

I blinked, unsure of what she meant by "everything." But there was something in her eye–a twinkle of amusement–that suggested she knew what I had done.

I took her hand and shook it. "Uh… don't mention it, happy I could help with the loan. Don't forget my discount!"

She chuckled and nodded. "I won't. There is little I will forget from this day."

# CHAPTER 9: WOULD NOT HESITATE

Our room at the Black Moon Inn was large, well-furnished, and very dusty. We appeared to be the only ones staying at the inn, for we encountered no one as we followed the old bushy-browed clerk up to our room. He pointed out the privy down the hall and explained that meals could be brought to the room upon request. We were charged three silver shimmers a night, which was triple what Sharla or Tammy had charged. I wondered why Maeve suggested the place, but maybe it was because of the lack of customers and foot traffic that Harkness and his cronies would not think to find us here, if he truly did intend us harm.

After checking in and seeing the room, we headed back to Sharla's to collect our wagon. Somehow she had already heard about the incident at Maeve's and gave us each a hug upon our arrival and then congratulated us on becoming inn owners, although we had yet to sign the title transfer and pay our final dues.

We collected our wagon from Sharla's stablehand and then made our way back to Southbank. The Black Moon Inn did not have a place to keep our wagon and so we stopped there first to unload some of our belongings, including a heavy chest, before finding a place to hold our horse and wagon.

Charm and I carried the chest together to our room. It wasn't so large or heavy that it was necessary for us to share the load, but we made a show of it in case anyone was watching. The case held only smooth obsidian shards that we had found on our journey here. They made a similar enough rattle to real coin that any onlooker or burglar would think it held the sum of our funds. But we had not faced such an issue yet in the small towns we'd stayed at during our journey.

Besides the coin purse Charm carried, the bulk of what I now knew to be a small fortune was stored in a secret compartment in the base of our wagon. Several runes were set up on it that would activate and cause all sorts of trouble if they were not properly deactivated first before opening the hatch. But the stable we found that could house our oversized wagon was several blocks away from the inn, and I worried if something was to go awry we would be too far from the wagon to reach it in time.

"Do you think it'll be safe?" I said to Charm as we walked back to the inn.

"It would have been safer if you had not so carelessly thrown about your funds in front of that criminal."

"What difference does that make? They know we're carrying enough coin to buy a tavern."

"That's not the issue," Charm said. "It is how carelessly you gave it away without even a contract. It suggests you consider the given sum insignificant."

I rubbed my chin and thought about it. It was in fact true that I had not thought much of the forty brilliances I'd given Maeve as it was only a small fraction of what Emdark had given me.

"I could also just be a fool who easily spends his rich merchant family's money," I offered.

Charm nodded. "That would not be far from the truth."

I gave her a scowl, even if I had opened the gate for that retort.

"You still haven't given me a direct answer," I said grumpily. "Is the wagon safe or not, Charm?"

Charm was the one to give me a dark look now. She still hadn't accepted her name. She turned her head back to the road as she spoke in her usual neutral voice, "Besides the sibling runes you set to inform of tampering, I also set a series of runes. Unless the thief is a perceiver and a runemaster, they'd be rendered obsolete before they touched a single coin."

"Rendered obsolete? Good Celeru, just what kind of runes did you set!"

"Elder runes," Charm said simply.

"Which ones?"

"Would you like me to teach them to you?" Charm said in a tone that suggested a challenge.

I looked away. "Not necessary," I replied, despite my deep desire. But I knew I could not accept, as it would only further weaken our bond. I could not allow her to become my teacher or any role that would question what we were.

"What did you think of the inn?" I said, hoping to lighten the mood.

Charm arched a brow at me. "What makes you think I have such thoughts at all? The inn means nothing to me. My only opinion is that this entire venture is foolish, if not fatally perilous. You have relinquished your magic and immortality. And by doing so I am also placed in disadvantage. We are susceptible to death just as much as any person here. The only difference is we have enemies that could destroy this city with a single incantation. Do you not see the precarious situation you've put us in?"

"The fact we are powerless is exactly why we are safe. No one knows who we are, and they will never be able to know, given our present states."

"Torren knows who you are."

"That won't happen again," I said.

"There are no such certainties. And the risks are too great."

I sighed. "What's the use dwelling on what's already done? This is where we are now. You know what it took for me to close my gates. I don't plan on giving that up any time soon, and that's assuming I even have the choice now."

Charm shook her head. "If you think I will accept a master on such a mindless path, then you know me not at all."

My steps came to a halt and I stared after her in shock, feeling the sudden cold weight in my chest. Never had she so openly threatened our bond.

Charm did not pause her stroll and after a moment I followed after her. With no more words to say, we walked the rest of the way in silence, and it stayed that way for the rest of the day. Our meals were eaten without words and as were our walks around the ward. I found Southbank to be fun and lively with colorful boutiques and many fine restaurants and taverns, and cafes. But whenever I looked over at Charm, I found no emotion on that placid face of hers. We retired early that night, and I lay in bed unable to sleep. Part of what kept me awake was the excitement of purchasing the tavern tomorrow. It would mean that I had finally achieved the first step of my dream. I thought of the brewing equipment on my wagon and the honey-flavored beer I dreamt of making.

The other half of me was filled with trepidation. What if Charm never came to accept our new way of life. What if she sought to take control of our bond? I felt my heart clench at the thought, for I knew it meant only one of us would survive such an event.

Then the question slipped into my mind.

*Could you kill her?*

The thought slipped away just as quickly as it came, for I knew the answer just as I knew myself. And I also knew if her decision was made, she would not hesitate either.

***

That night I dreamed of my father. We stood on the surface of a still lake beneath night stars. He smiled at me with kind eyes and asked, "How are you, my boy?"

I was surprised to find myself here again. It had been a long time since I last dreamt of him. So long that I could barely remember. But now that I was here, I felt the familiarity of the place and my father's presence.

"I am well," I said and found it to be true. "To-morrow I am buying the tavern."

"The tavern!" my father said, overjoyed. "Your long-held dream is finally coming true. Your master would be proud, as I am. But..." he had paused, looking deeply into my face. "Something troubles you."

"It's nothing," I said. I did not wish to discuss that subject with him. It wasn't a topic to broach in this peaceful place.

"You worry for your companion," he ventured.

I shook my head. That was far too much of a positive spin on the situation.

My father smiled at me. "She will enjoy herself as much as you will once the tavern is open, I am certain of it."

I sighed and looked out to the stars. My father followed my gaze and we sat quietly together until the dream ended and I woke in the dark room of the Black Moon Inn.

Blue light was just beginning to peek through the curtains. I turned in my blankets and looked across the room to Charm's bed. She was asleep, her head turned away from me.

Some strange emotion within me compelled me to whisper her name.

"Charm..."

I wanted to speak to her, but I thought of nothing to say. We were what we were and words alone could not change that. She did not stir.

# CHAPTER 10: ENTRUSTED

I paid Maeve a hundred and eight brilliances for the inn, and I paid four gold brilliances in the way of administrative fees to the city. Then the inn was signed to my name. By that transfer, I was granted immediate citizenship in the city of Meritas. After we had completed the contract and payment, Maeve invited us to eat with her. She and Albert took us to a tiny restaurant on the very southern edge of the ward. It was located beside a canal and had a nice view of the opposing bank and its many red brick buildings that warmed under the setting sun.

The kitchen took up most of the interior of the small restaurant, and we were seated at one of the four tables on the patio. The waiter brought us fresh bread, salted oil, and a jug of red wine. Then Maeve ordered what sounded like a feast for double the size of our party. We first talked of small pleasantries as we dipped our bread and nibbled on pickled mushrooms, cheese-stuffed olives, and smoked fish. Then when the main courses arrived, we began to speak of the events of the previous day. To my surprise, it was Charm who opened the topic.

"Pardon my curiosity," she said during a lull in conversation. "Has there been any news from the ward guard?"

"Did Captain Kainlin not inform you?" Albert said with surprise.

Charm and I both shook our heads.

Maeve frowned. "He should have. You were the one who was aggrieved. I ran into Kainlin's lieutenant at the market earlier today. Fine young woman. She took the time out of her patrol to give me the latest. They haven't found Sard, but Super-intendent Greengrass called Harkness to his office and gave him a browbeating. I would not have believed it if it hadn't come from the lieutenant herself. Few people are brave enough to stand up to Harkness, but I guess our ward superintendent is one of them."

I put my forked slice of pork chop back down and leaned over the table with interest. "What did the superintendent say to Harkness?"

"Told him that his men aren't welcome anymore in Southbank. Apparently that notary is an old friend of Greengrass' and gave the superintendent a full account of what happened. Shocked the living wits out of him. Not the lieutenant's words, but what I gathered from what she shared. Harkness claims Sard left his organization months ago, and that he had nothing to do with what happened. Greengrass didn't buy it and told Harkness Sard would be captured and questioned, and anyone who was involved would get sent to the magistrate with a maximum recommended sentence from the superintendent himself."

"Wow," I said. "Sounds like we should be lucky to have such a superintendent."

Maeve twisted her mouth. "He's got his blindspots, but he did more than anyone expected in this matter."

Albert smiled. "I wonder what he would have done if the magistrate's notary wasn't there."

"Likely the same," Maeve said. "Southbank's gearing up to be the city's newest commercial district. Can't have murders happening about, Harkness' involvement or not."

"That sounds like very good news for the ward," I said. "If true, your inn likely would have been alright if you could have hung on for a while longer."

Maeve grinned and waved her hand. "It's not the life for us anymore. Time my grandson and I took that trip we've always talked about."

"Young Albert informed us you were once an adventurer," Charm said politely.

Maeve nodded. "A long time ago. I even belonged to the guild at one point, turning in quests and traveling the continent. My daughter followed in my footsteps and met her husband, who was a fine swordhand. Shortly after Al was born, a friend offered them work as caravan guards. Low pay, but part of the offer came with letting them ride their own wagon. Convenient when you've got a young child. Not many adventuring jobs offer that sort of thing."

Maeve paused and her face tinged ever so slightly with sorrow. I noticed that Albert still kept his pleasant smile. It seemed the boy had come to terms with what happened next.

"Caravan jobs are usually safe. Especially a big one like the one they joined up on. Bandits don't raid guarded merchant caravans. Not worth fighting trained warriors. But that morning there'd been a heavy fog, and the bandits figured they had a chance to pull a fast one." Maeve shook her head. "Damned fools. They all died trying to take the caravan. But so did my daughter and son-in-law."

"They were heroes," Albert said proudly. "None of the merchants or travelers were injured."

"The adventurer's life isn't one for a child," Maeve said. She smiled fondly at her grandson. "But Al isn't a child anymore."

"Will you teach him to be an adventurer?" I said.

Maeve chuckled. "We'll travel Visseria and I'll teach him what I know. Then maybe we'll settle down somewhere quiet. Maybe even open another inn."

Albert rubbed his head. "If we do, I sure hope we have a finer showing for it."

Maeve swatted him lightly on the shoulder and we all laughed. Well, all of us except for Charm, who only nodded.

I raised my glass. "To your adventure," I said.

The others raised their glasses, and Maeve said, "To yours as well."

I smiled and tried to catch Charm's eye. But she did not look at me. Her gaze was focused on her wine.

***

The next morning we headed to the inn to meet with Maeve and Albert one last time. The inn was empty as ever, but it appeared the remaining belongings of the two had been stuffed into traveling packs that had been left by the door when we entered. Albert smiled and waved us a greeting as he came down the stairs. He was dressed in proper traveling clothes, leather boots, road belt, and all. But the boy looked tired and his eyes reddened as if from lack of sleep.

"Where's your grandmother?" I said.

"Ah..." Albert smiled sheepishly, rubbing the back of his head. "She's saying goodbye to the inn one last time."

We stood in an awkward silence for a time before we heard footsteps coming up the cellar stairwell. Maeve was holding an old sword, and I was surprised to find tears in the old adventurer's eyes. Then I realized that Albert's red eyes were likely from crying as well. I looked at both of them, feeling some unease.

"Are you alright?" I said to Maeve. I hoped she wasn't going to ask for her inn back at the last moment.

"Yes, of course," Maeve said gruffly. Then she held out the sword clutched in her hands. "This is for you."

I stared at the old sword, then back up at her. "I can't take your sword. You'll probably want it on your journey."

Maeve shook her head. "This isn't mine. It's the inn's. It was found buried here when the foundation was dug up. It's been here ever since. May it protect you and the inn."

I hesitated, then accepted the sword from her hands. I nearly flinched as my fingers wrapped around the sheath and hilt. Something about it felt terribly wrong in my hands. The wooden sheath was rough with age and yet had not molded. Instead, it looked nearly petrified. *Just how old is this thing?* I wondered. Then I noticed the symbols on the guard. An imperial seal. I nearly dropped the sword upon recognizing it. I had seen such a seal once before on a chest at the bottom of the sea. This sword wasn't just old, it was millennia old. Only then did I look up and realize that Maeve had been speaking, giving instruction on how to care for various parts of the tavern. I had not heard any of it but Charm had been nodding along.

I thought to return the sword to Maeve, for a sword of the One Empire was worth great value, but there was a wrongness to the sword that prevented me from giving it back to her. I did not understand it except that it felt foul. Had Maeve and Albert sensed it? Was that the reason they were crying? For they knew this item was what had brought them bad luck?

But both of them had not looked at the sword or seemed put off by it. Perhaps it was just my imagination.

Maeve's instructions came to an end. She gave one last look at the tavern.

"Well," she said, "It's been a ride. Good luck to you and your stewardship."

I was more than a steward, I was an owner. But I didn't say that. Instead I thanked them and smiled. "We'll take good care of her."

Maeve snorted and gave a nod. "I have a sense you will, and that brings ease to my heart."

She gave a low bow to Charm and I, then threw on her travel bag. Albert did the same and added, "We'll try to visit if we end up in Meritas again!"

"Please do, and a safe journey to you both," I said.

Charm returned their bow. "Safe travels."

Maeve turned to push open the door, then she paused and turned back. "I forgot to ask you. What shall you name it?"

Charm raised a brow and turned to me as did Albert.

I grinned at them all. "The Tipsy Pelican Tavern."

Maeve laughed. "What a silly name." Then she nodded her head. "I think it is perfect. Thank you, Arch."

With that, the two stepped out, leaving just Charm and I. We stood in silence for a time, then Charm said, "There is something evil about that sword."

"You sense it too."

Charm arched a brow at me.

"Well, I can't just toss it," I said. "They entrusted it to us,"

"That sword will draw misfortune, it is no wonder they kept it hidden."

"You think they knew something was wrong with it?"

Charm shook her head. "Not beyond instinct."

I sighed. "I'll put it in the cellar for now."

Charm said nothing, but she followed me into the cellar where I set the sword against a wall beside the stairwell. Even without touching it, I could sense its wrongness. But it was a problem to worry about at a later time.

My eyes wandered across the walls. I smiled at the enormous space, dry and odored with red brick, it was finally real. The Tipsy Pelican Tavern was a real place.

"We've got our work cut out for us, Charm," I said as my mind swam in imagination. "First we'll need to repaint the place, then get furniture, and build out the brewery." I laughed beside myself and Charm's placid gaze. "We have a tavern."

There was the sound of the main hall's door opening upstairs, and I looked up at the ceiling as it creaked with footsteps. "They must have forgotten something."

But when we came back up the cellar stairs, it was not Maeve and Albert that stood in my tavern.

Harkness smiled thinly at me beneath his mask. "Congratulations."

# CHAPTER 11: UNSUBTLE SUBTLETIES

I didn't like what I saw. The men that stood behind him had looks of ready violence. Then there was the way that Harkness held himself. Gone was the self-satisfied smile and in its place was a poor imitation held by the tight corners of his mouth. That same tightness was found in his shoulders and the way his hands folded into each other.

"So, it appears you've settled on a property," he said, keeping his tone casual.

I made a show of looking nervously over his shoulder and at the faces of his men. "S-ard isn't with you, is he?"

The smile tightened further into a thin line. "No. He is no longer acquainted with me." He paused momentarily and his voice went soft and cold. "Or anyone, for that matter."

"Oh dear," I said with a gasp. "So he really did lose his mind. But surely he still knows friend from foe."

"He never lost that," Harkness said, and his tone softened again, taking on that cold edge. "Not even at the end."

I waved my hand in disagreement. "I mean no disrespect in saying this, but you didn't see him at the time. The man clearly went mad. I just hope the ward guard find him before he does something else and then perhaps the healers can give him the treatment he needs to recover himself."

"There's no use treating a dead man."

"Don't say that! The ward guards aren't going to hang him for an affliction of the mind. Especially when nothing irreparable has come of it. I'm well enough, no harm done, and I can vouch for him if need be."

Harkness' cheek twitched as the opaque eyes of his mask seemed to watch me openly. An awkward tension was building in Harkness' men. One big guy behind Harkness shook his head and looked away, and another was shuffling his feet. Probably because their boss was trying to be all ominous and subtle in conveying he'd killed his own man. But that only works if the person you're trying to be subtle with understands what you're saying. Because if they don't, then you might have to keep hinting and do a lot of rewording and explaining, which will kill all that ominousness right fast.

"The ward guard aren't the ones who claimed his life," Harkness said finally.

I nodded to his comment with a show of grudging respect. "That's well said. We're in the Kingdom of Adentris after all. Our freedom was won by King Kindelore himself. No man can lay claim to our lives but ourselves."

Something was throbbing on Harkness' face now. He just stood there and glared at me, while most of the men behind him had suddenly taken a keen interest in the wood grain of the walls and ceilings.

But then Harkness smiled, and this time it seemed genuine. "A similar tactic you used against, Sard. He told me you forced his hand and conjured up the entire scenario. I thought he was lying to excuse his mistake. I even visited your old friend Torren for a true account of you. It seems I underestimated your cunning. But that's no reason for my right-hand man to be outsmarted. And for that, I had no choice but to end his service."

"Uh... who's Torro?"

"Torren, Tam's old man. At least in that you weren't lying. The old fool appears to have lost his wits."

"That geezer? I already told you I didn't know him."

Harkness shrugged. "A shame. I thought to charge you a life of a friend for costing me Sard's. But I suppose we shall have to settle that debt again another time."

I suddenly did not feel like fooling around anymore. Harkness laughed at the change in expression on my face.

"It was almost believable," he said, "by that look you're giving me. Those eyes. Almost. But you're nothing more than a gateless boy with more wits than is fair, but not enough to recognize your betters."

"What's almost believable?"

"What Torren said," Harkness said with another laugh. "When I asked him who you were, he told me, Archibold Stormblood. Can you believe it? Archibold Stormblood. It's funny enough, but humor is only humorous when it is properly timed." Harkness' grin dropped. "And that was not a time to jest."

I said nothing.

"I'll get to the crux of the matter then," Harkness said. "And this time, I'll make it very clear so you don't have another one of your misunderstandings." He lifted a finger at me. "You work for me now, Mr. Gustkin. You owe me for this inn that would have been rightfully mine if not for your interference. You owe me for the man I had to dump in the Central Canal. You owe me for the scrutiny of Southbank's superintendent, a relationship that I will now have to spend much time to rebuild. When you've worked off what you've cost me, you'll be free to leave. At that time, you'll transfer the property to me. But until then, I own you. And if you disobey me..." Harkness paused and turned his head ever so slightly toward Charm. "There is someone I am certain you are truly acquainted with."

In the end, the guy still couldn't come out and make his subtle threat direct despite promising to be clear. But it didn't seem like the right time to point that out. So instead, I said, "Apologies, but that makes no sense to me."

Harkness flashed me a smile again, and this time it was one of his casual, self-satisfied ones. "You will understand soon enough. People always do in the end."

With those parting words, he and his men took their leave.

# CHAPTER 12: WRECKAGE

I watched Harkness and his troop turn around the bend from the window. Then I caught Charm's gaze. She was frowning.

I held up a hand. "I know what you want to say. Now are you coming with me or would you prefer to stay here?"

Charm looked away but nodded and followed me out the door. We headed to the stable where we had kept our wagon and horse. I paid the stable master a silver shimmer for the rental and fitting of a saddle. Then I pulled myself onto Turtle, who shifted and neighed, seemingly unused to the weight coming from directly above. But she settled soon enough and I held out my hand to Charm.

She hesitated briefly before taking my hand, sliding up behind me.

We took to the roads at a fair pace and it was not before long that we reached Tammy's inn. Or what was left of it.

The glowing windows and inviting aromas of a fine chef were replaced by a heap of burnt timber and drifting ash. Several laborers were sorting the wreckage, pushing the dust and blackened wood fragments off the main road.

I pulled up to the nearest one and hailed him. "Beg your pardon," I said. "What happened here?"

The man looked up and gave me a look that nearly belonged to Charm. "What happened? What does it look like happened?"

He spoke his words like a man who'd been asked the question too many times.

"I'm looking for the owner of this inn," I said.

His demeanor softened and he nodded down the road. "The innkeeper's at the healer's clinic. It's just a few blocks down, you shan't miss it... my condolences."

I thanked the man and turned Turtle around and in the direction the man had directed. Sure enough, we found the healer's clinic after three blocks, a modest building with a faded but easily recognizable sign.

At the clerk's desk we gave Tammy's name and identity and the healer on duty led us to a tiny room with two cots. One was empty and Tammy lay in the other. She did not look to have many burns as only her left arm was bandaged, but her eyes were closed with a deep wrinkle in her brow that not even unconsciousness could release.

"How is she?" I said to the healer.

The healer shook her head. "She breathed many fumes and it has caused injuries internally. She was looked at by our chief, but even he is only capable of minor healing magic. Her recovery will take much time. She has woken a few times but spoken little."

I knew Charm could heal her easily, but I could not ask her. "Couldn't you give her a potion?" I said.

The healer shook her head again. "No family has come forth to offer to pay the costs to obtain such a potion from an alchemist. They are expensive things, and we must reserve the few donated to us by the duke for those on the brink of life and death."

"What about her grandfather?" I said. "He also worked at the inn."

"I'm afraid we did not receive any other patients from the fire... perhaps you could check with the ward guard?"

I said nothing after that and the healer gave a short bow, leaving us to attend to other duties. I stared out the window, not looking at Tammy. After a time, I said, "Let's go."

But before we headed out the door, I heard a croak of a voice. "M-ister Gustkin..."

I turned and saw Tammy staring up at me through slitted eyes.

"Tammy," I said, stepping to her bed.

"Oh, Mister Gustkin..." Tammy's voice trembled as she spoke.

"Tell me what happened."

She gave an almost imperceptible nod and her eyes cleared a little. "H-Harkness demanded to speak to Grandda. They took him out back and beat him... Grandda told them... he told them you were the Stormblood, that Harkness better leave you alone. I don't know why he said that. It made Harkness mad and he hit him again and again. There was nothing I could do but watch. It was horrible... horrible..." Tammy paused here, her eyes becoming wet and distant suddenly, as if reliving the events once more.

"What happened next?" I said.

Tammy turned her eyes toward me, but they were still far away. "He ordered his men to set fire to my tavern. One of his men had gagged me, and they took off the gag so I could scream to my patrons and staff. I told them to run. I screamed until I was hoarse, then someone hit me on the back of the head. When I woke again, Grandda was beside me. He had crawled to me. I can still see the fire light on his face, and the shadows. Harkness was gone." Tammy's eyes focused now. She was staring at me intently. "Why did he say such things? Why is Harkness so interested in you?" Her voice cracked with pain and confusion.

"I am sorry for your loss," Charm said.

Tammy didn't seem to have heard her. "Grandda told me it was nice seeing you one last time. And he... he said that you would make things right. It was the last thing he said to me... I know you aren't who he thinks you are... I know... but... but..." Tears welled up in Tammy's eyes. "They killed him, Mr. Gustkin. They killed him and no one will do anything about it."

"Have you spoken to the ward guard?" I asked, hoping for some semblance of justice.

Tammy shook her head. "He owns this ward's superintendent. Owns him good, it's said. They all know Harkness was behind this. They won't... come to speak to me..."

Her last words were a whisper. Exhaustion took her as her eyes clouded over again as she fell back into unconsciousness.

I watched her for a long moment before I took my leave of the clinic. I did not look at Charm as I stepped outside. Too many thoughts rang loudly in my mind and I did not need her look of disapproval to worsen them.

Neither of us seemed in the mood to share the saddle and so we walked silently as we led Turtle back the way we came, passing the remains of the inn. The once lively place was now a charred skeleton of what it had been, and somehow that weighed heavily on me. The scent of smoke seemed to linger around me even after we had long left the area.

"What will you do?" Charm said finally as the tavern came into sight.

"What can I do?" I said to myself more than to Charm. "I'm just a tavern keeper now."

There was a long pause, then Charm said, "Arch."

"Yeah?" I said, awaiting some rebuke.

"Look." She pointed past over my shoulder toward our newly purchased tavern. There was a man painting a large red cross on the front door.

"Hey!" I exclaimed, letting go of the reins and rushing toward him.

The man spotted me coming and threw his brush back in the bucket, but he did not run. He simply ignored my calls and walked away from the tavern at a leisurely pace.

"Stop there! You've committed a crime!"

He ignored me and there were no ward guards or passerby that came to my aid.

A hot rage flashed within me, but I pushed it away. There were a few pedestrians on the street and I could not afford an altercation so soon after becoming a citizen. But beyond that, I was a warrior no more.

"Wait!" I called after him.

The man continued walking, ignoring me as he had to all my other shouts.

"Tell Harkness I'll pay him for the tavern!"

This put a halt to his steps. He turned and smiled. There was a thick scar that ran around the corner of his mouth. It curved with the line of his lips. "You say something, boy?"

"You heard me," I said. "Tell him to come to my tavern tonight. We'll settle it then."

The man's grin widened, but he said nothing and continued on his way.

I heard Charm come up behind me with the horse. I turned to her and said, "Take Turtle and bring the wagon around. Then go to the stables outside the city and get a good price for him. He's served us well, but we can't keep him."

Charm's eyes narrowed. "Why must I go outside the city?"

"Because you'll fetch a better price there, and because you'll take a long time."

"You don't want me here when Harkness comes."

"He included you in his threat."

"He can do nothing to me."

"I'm more afraid of what you'd try to do to him."

"You truly intend to pay him off, then."

"What other choice do I have?"

An expression formed on Charm's face. It was the first since we arrived in the city. It was a look of disgust. "I am bound to an imbecile."

I frowned bitterly. "So you are. Now go."

# CHAPTER 13: AS AGREED

Charm did not speak to me when she returned with the wagon. She unhitched Turtle and led him away without even looking at me as I came out of the tavern. I sighed heavily and wondered to myself just how long our tavern would last. Or if it would even begin. But I went about unpacking our wares and bringing our things into the inn.

We had few personal effects in the wagon, as most of our cargo consisted of machinery and brewing equipment. Much of the former went upstairs and the latter into the cellar. The sun was setting by the time I had finished unloading everything. Even then the inn still felt empty. There was much work to be done before it could be considered a true tavern.

While unloading, I had come across a bottle of Elven brandy that had been given to me as a gift. In the kitchen, I found a bowl that Maeve and Albert had left behind and filled it halfway. Then I sat on the steps in the main hall and sipped on the liquor. It was the very good stuff, the best in fact. But I found I had no taste for the drink and it did little to ease the heavy weight in my heart.

I thought of all the events that had brought me to this moment. I finally had a tavern of my own, just as I had dreamed for so long, and yet I felt little joy. My companion was upset with me and now there was a criminal that could ruin the whole thing before I even opened my doors for business.

*Is this really what I want?* I asked myself. *Is it even worth it?*

Maeve seemed to think so. She had been willing to sacrifice everything to keep the tavern out of Harkness' hands. When she could no longer run the tavern profitably herself, she'd sold everything of value in the tavern to pay off the interest on his debts while she searched for a suitable buyer. Even the furniture and the locks on the room doors. And when that had not been enough, she seemed ready to lay down her life. I didn't understand it. Sure, I wanted a tavern for the fun of it, but I could not see the place ever being a reason to throw away my life.

I heard the creak of a window being pushed open and the unlatching of a lock. It appeared to come from the kitchen. Then came the steps of men entering from the kitchen's backdoor, they were coming in from the alley behind the inn. Outside the main hall's windows, I saw it had become dark and the street empty.

The men shuffled through the corridor and into the main hall. There were a dozen of them and Harkness was the last to step into the lamplight of the hall.

"Pleasant of you to call," he said. "I had intended to pay you a visit soon enough."

I stood, matching his height, and looked across the faces of the men he had brought. Then I returned my gaze to the crystalline eyes of his mask.

"This is my offer," I said, "I will pay you what I gave Maeve for this property. There is no fairer price than that for your troubles. In return, I ask that you leave me be and never step foot into my tavern again."

Harkness smiled but shook his head. "A hundred and fifty gold brilliances is the price Maeve charged you for this inn. But that was her price. As this inn was rightfully mine, you must pay my price."

"And what would that be?"

Harkness looked around as if evaluating its value, then returned to face me. "I think three hundred and fifty brilliances is a fair asking price for such a fine establishment."

I winced but gave the bigger shock when I held out my hand to him. "I trust you are man of your word."

Harkness stared at me, then let out a laugh and took my hand. "I suppose we all would have benefited from being born a rich merchant's son. We have a deal. Now show me to the gold."

I led them down into the cellar. The room still felt massive even with my brewing equipment carefully placed in crates at a far corner. Against the back wall was where I had left the chest. I had taken out the stones and replaced them with the gold that we had hidden in the wagon.

Without looking backward, I stepped up to the chest and withdrew a leather coin wrap from my trouser pocket. Then I opened the chest and began counting out three hundred and fifty gold brilliances. As I counted, I felt Harkness' men drawing closer around me. I ignored them and double checked my count. Then I tied the leather and turned, holding the payment out to him.

"Three hundred and fifty brilliances as agreed," I said.

No man, not even Harkness eyed the satchel in my hands.

"Gustkin," Harkness said in a voice that sounded almost sweet. "Just how much gold do you possess?"

"Enough to renovate and furnish the tavern. Your payment, sir." I extended the satchel hand further toward him.

Harkness shook his head. "I suspect you have a great deal more than that in your chest. But why show it to me? If you thought to inform me of your family's power and wealth, it was a mistake. Had I known you held enough to cover what you truly cost me, I would have given a more honest price."

I clenched my jaw. "You gave your word."

"True enough. I shall accept your payment for the inn." Harkness nodded and a large man stepped forward and snatched the leather satchel from my hand. "But you've also cost me the life of my right hand man," Harkness continued. "That is a debt we have yet to settle."

"Our agreement has already been made! You promised to leave me alone for that gold!" My voice sounded shrill even to my own ears.

"No one saw us when we entered," Harkness said, darkly.

"Y-you intend to rob me," I breathed.

Harkness spread his hands, smiling again. "I intend to take what I am owed."

The man who had taken the satchel took another step toward me, moving to push me out of the way.

I fell backward and pushed the chest closed. "Stay back! I'm warning you! Stay back!"

"Do not make this more difficult than it needs to be," Harkness said. "We are beneath ground and these walls are made of brick. No one will hear you. Hand over the chest and keep your life. Then I will leave you be."

At these words, the man with the satchel reached to grab my shoulder, but before his calloused hand could touch me, I drew the inn's sword from behind the chest. It slid from its sheath, flashing lamp light against its ancient steel.

The large man grinned incredulously at this, as if he were watching a child with a stick. He turned to show his disbelieving smile to the other men, who laughed at the shared joke. Then he moved toward me with a casual and confident grace, his mouth still curved and his eyes bright with humor right until my blade plunged into his belly.

# CHAPTER 14: A TRUE FOOL

T he man spluttered at me with disbelieving eyes before taking a faltering step and toppling to the floor, blood pooling out from beneath his body. The faces of the others darkened rapidly, some muttering curses as they drew knives and swords from their belts.

Harkness sighed. "That was unwise."

He drew back while the rest of his men shuffled toward me in a half circle. I ducked the first swing to arrive and lunged sideways against the wall, meeting the two men there head on. There would be no chance for me once the circle of opponents closed against the walls. The two men at the very end saw me coming and raised their swords to meet mine. I caught the first swing against my sword and dodged the second man's stab, kicking him in the hip as he passed me, but he did not fall, only grunting and taking three steps to catch his balance. I pushed away the first man's sword and leapt through the narrow opening where the second man had been. Rolling away, I turned quickly around, ready for the next strike. But the others hadn't swarmed after me. They moved cautiously, reforming the circle. They were taking their time, which was the worst possible scenario. I had hoped they'd be angry and reckless after the loss of one of their own. So I changed my tactics, darting forward first, striking at the man closest to me, three or four others stood disjointedly behind him. My blade met his twice and on the third I'd left him open for a deathblow on the fourth, but then someone else was at my side, roaring as his sword came crashing down beside me. I'd leapt away, missing my chance to reduce their numbers by another man. More of the men were arriving now, joining the attack. Something tore against my shoulder and I felt wetness before pain, but I had no time to check my wound as I blocked and weaved through the oncoming strikes. Three men slashed their blades at me while the others snuck around me to strike from behind.

Once again I leapt and rolled away, reaching the opposing wall. The only thing worse than being cornered was being surrounded. I threw my back against the brick as the closest thug followed after me. His weapon clanged against the wall when his strike missed and the rattle against his hands caught him by surprise. I pushed my blade into his unprotected chest and withdrew quickly as another swordsman arrived, his blade splitting the air where my head had been.

His second strike came heavy and fast, and I already felt myself tiring and the gnawing weakness of my shoulder. My body moved out of the way on its own, and Maeve's words rang in my mind. *Not while my heart's still beating,* she had said.

*And how long would I last?* I wondered.

The next blow came down heavy and I had to catch it with the support of my hand against the flat of the blade. The muscled brute pushed down hard with his weight, but I held him off until he released a hand from his sword that clenched into a fist. I was too slow and three of his knuckles caught me against the cheek, sending me flying to the side and landing hard on my back. Despite the patterns in my eyes and head, I held up my sword, feeling it batted away against the ground just as I did, there was no time for reprieve. In my darkened vision another man was already on me, making a downward chop mid run. I kicked his left foot from under him, offsetting his balance and sending him toppling past me. I pushed myself back onto my feet, still dazed from the punch, finding two more blades rushing toward my torso. I caught them both against my sword, then stepped backward, sensing footfalls behind me. I ducked for a strike, but felt a stab instead, a knife parting the muscle between my shoulders.

I pulled away from it, barely blocking another hack by the big brute from before. I pushed aside his blade and swung on him with all my might. He threw up his sword and my ancient blade shattered against his steel. He let out a cry as blade fragments caught him in the neck and face. I stumbled away with my broken sword until I felt my back touch again upon the cold cellar wall. The other attackers did not relent. I sank down as a blade chipped away brick from above. Four men were suddenly standing over me. I deflected one thrust but not the other, it caught me between the right ribs. I pulled away, feeling skin rip with the motion, I spun into the corner and the men followed me, huddling close like a pack of wolves around an injured doe, their eyes alight with blood thirst.

My sword was broken and my body was not far from becoming the same. I clutched tightly to the wound, breathing heavily. In the gaps between my opponents, I caught sight of Harkness. He stood well behind them, but there was a change in his posture. And then suddenly I knew she was there, even before she screamed.

"HAVE YOU GONE MAD!?"

All heads turned to the source of the voice. She stood at the base of the staircase, eyes filled with dark rage, and something ripped deep within my chest. I looked down, expecting to find a blade plunged there, but the tunic there was unscathed save for being drenched in sweat. Something was tearing against my soul.

Without taking his eyes off of Charm, Harkness snapped his fingers at me and the closest man batted away my broken sword as another grabbed me by the collar and put a blade against my neck. There would have been no strength left to resist.

"Your friend killed one of my men," Harkness said to Charm after noting I had been subdued. "Come down and let us talk. We still may yet let him live."

Charm's hateful gaze never left my eyes. *I said, have you gone mad?*

The words had been directed toward me. My chest, no, my very existence felt as if it were about to rip apart from within. I averted my gaze, for I had no words to give in reply.

"Indeed he has," Harkness said. "He kill-"

"*Close your face*," she growled in a voice so full of hate that Harkness flinched. Never had I felt such emotion from her before. I looked up to find that her eyes had not left me. *"Explain yourself before I destroy you all."*

In that moment, I suddenly felt like the fool she thought I was. Like a stupid child caught with a broken toy. My shoulders dropped and the tension in my body went limp. "I.. I was curious... that's all."

"*Curious?*" Charm said in a voice that made the word more an accusation than a question.

"The old adventurer would have given everything to defend this place..." I smiled without mirth. "It would have cost her life..." I shook my head. It felt heavy. "It would seem a common existence is not so easy either."

Something about my words shocked her, for the tearing pressure in my chest abated momentarily, but the frown on her face seemed eternal.

*"Then,"* she said, *"have you satisfied your curiosity?"*

Had I?

Perhaps as much as I could learn in such a short time. Maeve would have fought to the bitter end as Harkness' men swarmed around her. Even wounded, her sword broken, even with hope of justice gone, she would have gone down fighting, taking as many as she could with her. But in the end, Harkness would have won. I could see it now, I could almost feel the pain and anger she would have felt. But there was still something I didn't understand.

"I don't know why she would have made the sacrifice," I said to Charm. "But maybe, I shall learn that with time."

"Enough!" Harkness spat. "I've heard just about enough-"

I stuck my thumb into the wrist of the man holding the blade to my throat. My finger pressed away the tendon that made his grip and his sword fell into my open hand and I sheathed and drew it from his solar plexus. The three others beside me whose attentions had been caught by Charm's anger turned at the sound of his agony just as my swing took two of them by the neck. The third threw up a reflexive arm before it was severed from him along with part of his shoulder and clavicle. I felt my bones and muscles scream at my movements. It was not the same as when my body had been immortal. But my will held their complaints at bay as Harkness' men arrived and fell in flashes of red. I moved now without the restriction of an old adventurer, falling into old forms garnered from two centuries of violence. I thought I felt nothing as the bodies parted around me, their blood painting the cellar walls red. But as I dipped the sword point into the last of Harkness's men, I found that it was not true. I did feel something. Something that burned deep within me, so deep

I had not noticed it. I had thought such feelings had been lost to me long long ago. Then the town of Roundtree flashed before my eyes. It's clumsily built cabins and homes from wide circular blocks of yellow timber. The baker's straw hut and its ever-smoking chimney. The young boy seeing me through the window, eyes going wide with excitement and waving and calling out to me. "It's Mr. Stormblood! Mr. Stormblood has returned!" Then he was rushing out the door, running toward me with a fresh steaming loaf that looked far larger than it was in his small hands. Only then did I become aware I had planned for this bloody outcome all along. It would not have mattered if Harkness had accepted my payment. It would not have mattered if he had no intent to rob me. The goading of gold and opening of wounds had only been to assuage my conscience. *A true fool, I am.*

Harkness' mouth opened and shut beneath his mask. "Who- who are.."

Then the mask parted, revealing one clouding brown eye and the other white and clouded long before the blade in my hand had anything to do with it. He fell to his knees and then to the ground, leaking from his split face.

Charm came to stand beside me and I did not look for her expression, afraid of what I may find there. Would she chide me for my hypocrisy? Would she congratulate me? I wished for neither.

But when she said nothing, I asked her, "Do you wish to leave?"

She was silent for a long while and when I could not hold my curiosity any longer, I turned to her, finding that her frown was gone and she seemed lost in her own thoughts. Then her eyes closed and opened once and the frown returned. "Who am I to question another's path?" She murmured, more to herself than it seemed to me.

She faced me and put a hand lightly against my shoulder, not looking me in the eyes. "You are wound-" She paused then and shook her head as if coming to a decision.

For a long moment, I felt only her touch against my shoulder. Then she spoke again. And with those words, everything would change between us.

"Master is wounded. Shall Charm heal him?"

I stared at her with open disbelief. But like the sudden chime of a bright bell, the ripping, turbulent storm in my chest that had plagued me since our journey subsided into nothingness.

Charm finally met my gaze and her features had taken on its usual imperceptible placidity except for one ever so slightly raised eyebrow. "Well, Master?"

I nodded and felt wetness in my eyes. "Thank you, Charm."

# CHAPTER 15: THE PURPOSE

C harm wore a white linen summer dress and took a bite from her orange icicle on a stick as she walked, her gaze lifted placidly into the sky as if pondering some inquiring thought.

"Hey aren't you going to help me at all!" I exclaimed, nearly dropping the pull cart again. We were nearly there, but the sun was damned hot and my sweaty hands were having trouble holding onto the pull cart's smooth wood handles.

Charm turned toward me with an arch in her brow and a withering look in her eyes. Despite the understanding that had been reached between us, her cold demeanor toward me had not abated.

She had accepted my decision, but she still did not seem to enjoy any part of it.

"It is not Charm's fault Master ordered her to sell dear Turtle, who would have been much help in our current predicament."

She was right about that. I could count on all my hands and toes the number of times the horse would have come in handy in the past two weeks. Just the transporting of the furniture alone would have been a blessing. But I shook my head.

"Turtle's no draft horse," I said. "He's in a better place now."

Charm nodded, finishing the last bit of her icicle and returning her gaze to the sky. "Charm hopes the butcher does him honor."

"Who exactly did you sell him to!?"

Charm's shrug was almost imperceptible. "Charm was in a hurry."

"He was a natural traveler! A veteran of Visseria's roads! How could you!?"

"The butcher assured Charm Turtle would be put to good use for ferrying rune-frozen meats to and from Lareinti."

I gave her a flat look. "So you sold him to a merchant."

Charm chewed on the empty icicle stick. "A relevant memory has come to Charm. Horse meat is a delicacy in Lareinti, is it not?"

"So you did send him to his death!"

"Charm followed Master's orders."

"I should have had you sell yourself!"

"Perhaps another would have been sent to their death in such a case."

I shuddered, but despite her words, I felt no strangeness in my chest.

"Turtle is able and strong," Charm said. "Lareinti's tastes favor grassland horses. Master should not be worried in this matter. Rather, now that he is mortal, he should consider where he shall find his own sustenance, now that his coffers have been thoroughly emptied."

"What are you talking about?" I said. "We'll have revenues flowing in once the tavern opens in a fortnight."

"Opening a door does not ensure anyone shall step through. Especially when the owner of the door is a childish fool, the atmosphere past the door lacks music, and the ales on the counter are acceptable at best."

"I'm going to go ahead and ignore your first slight so that I can put all my attentions on the last one–the Honeydew lager turned out pretty darn good for a first try!"

"All men have their opinions…"

"I'd like to see you do a better job!"

"Charm remembers Master said he was very pleased with her stew."

She was right about that. If you told me the best stew I'd ever tasted was going to be cooked by Charm, I would have laughed in your face until the sun set and the moon hung and all the stars of the night were shining brightly, but indeed it was. Of course I'd never admit this to her. So instead

I gave a witty retort about the furniture that we had chosen, which was actually probably less of a retort and more of a changing of subjects. Charm seemed to have an arsenal of slights for that topic as well and so I was very happy indeed when we reached our destination. We were in the ward of Oakden, standing before a narrow shack with a crooked wooden door in an empty alley.

"This is definitely the place, right?"

"It is the address given by the clinic," Charm said. Then she eyed the chest in the cart. "Is Master certain this is a wise decision?"

"Wise? What does wise have to do with it?"

Charm nodded. "Charm does believe that statement summarizes Master's disposition quite well."

My eye twitched as I said, "My point is we aren't here in Meritas to be wise."

"Clearly. But that does not mean Master should avoid wisdom, intelligence, and all morsels of general good sense. Master has left himself no safety of funds, given the probability of his business success."

I shot her a scowl. "Look here. Have you ever played stones?"

"The game?"

"Yes, the game."

"Charm supposes she has, though it has been a time."

"Yes, but you remember how to play, don't you? Each person places a stone on the board until one player fully surrounds their opponent."

Charm nodded. One brow was arched.

I leaned toward her. "Have you ever played starting with most of your stones already on the board?"

Charm shook her head. "That would defeat the purpose."

I slapped the chest. "Exactly."

"Ah." Charm looked down at the chest. "And here Charm thought Master was performing an act of generosity, or at the very least, making a foolish attempt to alleviate his conscience."

"Don't be silly, does that sound like me?" I said. "Come on, help me get this thing out of the cart."

We carried the chest on each side and set it down quietly before the shack's doorstep. Then Charm retrieved an envelope from her bag and placed it on top of the chest.

"What's this?" I said, taking the envelope as she pulled out two more items, a candle and a match, from her bag. Charm did not respond, but she lit the candle with her match. She appeared to be waiting for me, and so I opened and read the letter within.

*Dear Tamantha Goodland,*

*It has come to my attention that criminals in my city have done great injustice toward you. I know what I offer you now is no consolation for the evil that has occurred, but know well the criminals responsible have been brought to justice. I ask that you do not share this missive with anyone else for reasons I cannot explain here. May you find hope in this city once more.*

*D.R.*

"D. R.?" I said. "Oh... I see. From the duke, huh? That's very clever."

I blinked and handed her the letter and envelope, which she sealed with wax from the candle. Then she opened the lid of the chest and slipped the letter inside. Turning the candle, she dripped more wax directly upon the top of the chest. With her forefinger, she drew a symbol that I did not recognize.

"What does that do?" I said.

"What do you think?" Charm said. "Charm does not wish for Master's half-hearted good deed to go toward the wrong benefactor."

So it was a rune that prevented the chest from being opened by anyone other than Tammy. But I did not understand how Charm could have bound it to the innkeeper. Neither did I have a chance of her answering such a question.

"Come on," I said with a sigh. "Let's get going before anyone sees us."

Charm joined me at my side as I pulled the empty cart back down the road.

"Hold on," I said suddenly as we made our way out of the alley and onto the main street. "Something is terribly wrong here."

"What is it, Master?"

"When did you write the letter? I didn't even plan to give her the rest of the gold until this morning. How could you have known?"

"It is because Charm is Charm."

"How is that an answer?"

Charm nodded. "Very well, the reason Charm knew what he would do from the very beginning is because Master is an itiut."

"Don't even start!" I snapped.

We argued the whole way back to our tavern.

*Volume End.*

# AFTERWORD

**H**ello friends,

(and welcome back to all my returning tavern regulars!)

This prequel was written with two purposes in mind: to introduce new readers to the *Tipsy Pelican Tavern* series and to give longtime fans some extra backstory to enjoy. Balancing both wasn't easy, but I hope it's been as fun to read as it was to write.

I'm also excited to share that the entire *Tipsy Pelican Tavern* series is getting a full rerelease. The new editions will feature updated professional artwork and refined prose that makes the story flow even better. Once Volumes 1–4 are reissued,

Volume 5 will follow. If you'd like to be notified the moment it releases, be sure to follow me on Amazon.

For audiobook listeners, the prequel and Volume 1 are already available. Narrators Joshua Story and Laurie Catherine Winkel have done an incredible job bringing the tavern to life with humor, heart, and distinct voices for each character. They truly captured the spirit of the series.

Here's what early listeners have said about the Volume 1 audiobook:

"The narrators Joshua and Laurie do a great job voicing the large cast of characters. I have to give Laurie props—she nailed exactly how I imagined Charm sounding when I read the book."

"Great story by the author and great performance by both speakers. Highly recommend this audiobook."

If you'd like to stay in the loop for updates, cover reveals, and sneak peeks, you can join my newsletter at www.august.art. With Volume 1's rerelease landing soon, now is the perfect time to sign up.

Thank you so much for reading and for supporting the tavern. Reviews are one of the best ways to help new readers discover the series, so if you enjoyed the story, I'd be deeply grateful if you left one.

And one last note—we now have a Reddit community at /r/TipsyPelicanTavern. It's a space to chat, share theories, and connect with other fans of the series. Stop by and say hi!

That's all for now. I'll see you in the next volume.

All the best,

**August Hei**

Special thanks to my amazing Patreon supporters:

MGeo, Bullet Philia, John W, Josh, Jemention, Will, Dale, Vic X, Jennie C., Chad A., Stephen M., Martin M, TC128, Dan A., Pipes M!

# TIPSY PELICAN TAVERN SUGGESTED READING ORDER

VOL 1: Even a Hero Needs a Vacation Every Now and Then

Prequel #1 - Elsa's Story: Sweat, Scoundrels, and Taverns

VOL 2: Everyone Knows You Shouldn't Rescue Maidens in Alleyways

Prequel #2 - Cassia's Story: The Final Test

Prequel #3 - Roddard's Story: A Road to Meritas

VOL 3: Rare Swords Are Only Good Until You Lose Them

VOL 4: You Can't Be an Assassin if You Have a Leather Allergy

**Read at any time:**

Tipsy Pelican Tavern : Origins

**Read the prequel short stories for free at:**

www.august.art

Get awesome Tipsy Pelican Tavern merch at: shop.august.art!

www.ingramcontent.com/pod-product-compliance
Lightning Source LLC
Chambersburg PA
CBHW072135300726
48975CB00003B/1072